"You're nearly always so controlled, Max."

Bethan went on quickly. "But I'm not sure I was right about you being cold. You pretend to be. Then something in your eyes gives you away."

"You might not like it if I did ever lose control," Max warned softly, and his eyes suddenly glittered.

"But you like blondes," she reminded him, an edge now in her voice as she thought of his fiancée. "Look at me. Black hair, dark eyes—I'm definitely not your type, Max."

"Wrong, Bethan. Right now, you look *exactly* my type."

With a brief, impatient movement, he bent his head and inflicted a kiss on her that was rough and yet totally pleasurable.

The third kiss, Bethan told herself dazedly. She had wondered about it—but she couldn't possibly have known what it would do to her.

JOANNA MANSELL finds writing hard work but very addictive. When she's not bashing away at her typewriter, she's usually got her nose buried in a book. She also loves gardening and daydreaming, two pastimes that go together remarkably well. The ambition of this Essex-born author is to write books that people will enjoy reading.

Books by Joanna Mansell

HARLEQUIN PRESENTS
1116—MIRACLE MAN
1139—LORD AND MASTER
1156—ILLUSION OF PARADISE

HARLEQUIN ROMANCE
2836—THE NIGHT IS DARK
2866—SLEEPING TIGER
2894—BLACK DIAMOND

Don't miss any of our special offers. Write to us at the following address for information on our newest releases.

Harlequin Reader Service
901 Fuhrmann Blvd., P.O. Box 1397, Buffalo, NY 14240
Canadian address: P.O. Box 603,
Fort Erie, Ont. L2A 5X3

JOANNA MANSELL

the third kiss

Harlequin Books

TORONTO • NEW YORK • LONDON
AMSTERDAM • PARIS • SYDNEY • HAMBURG
STOCKHOLM • ATHENS • TOKYO • MILAN

Harlequin Presents first edition July 1989
ISBN 0-373-11186-X

Original hardcover edition published in 1988
by Mills & Boon Limited

CHAPTER ONE

BETHAN was very cold and very thirsty. But more than that, she was beginning to get extremely frightened. When she had set out this morning, she had had no idea her Egyptian holiday was going to turn into this sort of nightmare.

She stared at the bleak, barren landscape that lay in front of her, its very starkness giving it a strange beauty. Lit only by the pale glow of the huge moon overhead, it seemed unreal, and terrifyingly devoid of all life. Valley of the Kings—site of the magnificent tombs of the long-dead Pharaohs of Egypt. Such a romantic name for such a desolate place. And she was beginning to wonder if it was going to turn out to be her last resting-place, as well.

Oh, stop being so morbid! she told herself angrily. Someone from the tour party is eventually going to realise you're missing, and then they'll get up a search team. You'll be found in no time.

But in the meantime she was stuck here on this cliff-top, unable to scramble down again because of her injured knee. How long had she been here? Hours, she supposed, because the sun had been beating down fiercely when she had first tackled the climb. Now, the moon had taken the place of the sun, so big and so bright that it didn't seem possible there couldn't be some warmth in those pale rays. Yet there wasn't, and she was shivering deeply now because this was a desert region, where the heat of the day gave way at night to a bone-chilling cold.

She wrapped her arms around herself, sitting in a tight huddle now as she tried to keep warm. Just keep calm, she told herself shakily. They'll come looking for you soon; all you've got to do is hang on a bit longer and not panic. The trouble was, that was easy to say but definitely not easy to do. She couldn't help wondering what would happen if they *didn't* come. What if she was stuck here all night, and then all day tomorrow? And perhaps even the day after that?

Bethan lifted her head in a defiant gesture. 'Don't be such a pessimist!' she muttered out loud. 'You're going to be rescued, and everything's going to turn out all right. You *are* going to be rescued,' she repeated to herself very firmly.

As if in miraculous response to her words, something moved in the valley below. Bethan blinked disbelievingly, and leant forwards a little. For a few moments, she thought it had just been wishful thinking and she had imagined it. Then the dark shape moved again, crossing a patch of sand illuminated by the silvery moonlight, so she could clearly see a tall figure.

She let out a whoop of relief. Then she yelled as loud as she could, and began to wave her arms.

The figure stopped and half turned. It was a man, his head lifting attentively as he tried to work out where the shouting was coming from.

'Up here,' she yelled, her voice echoing clearly on the still night air. She leant perilously close to the edge of the cliff and flailed her arms around frantically. 'Hey—I'm up here!'

She was sure he had seen her; he seemed to be looking straight at her now. Then he switched his attention to the steep slope she had climbed earlier, studying it carefully, as if trying to decide which was the safest route up. Bethan tried to contain her impatience. It wasn't a difficult climb—if she hadn't twisted her stupid knee, she would have been able to get down again quite easily. Then she reminded herself that she had tackled it in daylight. It was dark now, which would make it much more difficult because he wouldn't be able to see the loose stones and treacherous patches of scree.

Finally, the man began to climb. Bethan's eyes brightened with excitement as she watched him move quickly and easily, as if he had scaled far more difficult rock-faces than this one. In just minutes, he had reached the top. Then he was standing only inches away, looming over her, tall, commanding and, now that he was close to her, more than a little forbidding.

His gaze raked over her. 'How the *hell* did you get up here? Only an idiot would try and climb a cliff like this.'

Bethan instantly bristled. There was no need for him to adopt that tone!

'Never mind how I got up here,' she said, her own voice sharp with nerves. 'More to the point, how are you going to get me down again?'

'Take that kind of attitude, and I might not bother,' he told her coolly.

Panic instantly washed over her, and she grabbed hold of his hand. 'I'm sorry,' she gabbled, 'I didn't mean to be rude. It's just that I've been so scared. I've been stuck up here for hours, and I was beginning to think no one was ever going to come . . .' Her voice ran out and she swallowed nervously. Then she realised she was still clinging slightly frantically to his hand. It felt warm and firm against her fingers, something solid to hang on to. She didn't want to let go, but was starting to feel a little embarrassed now. Slowly, she unlocked her fingers and released her grip on him. She took a deep breath, deliberately steadying herself, and then lifted her head to look up at him.

'It's all right, I'm not going to get hysterical,' she assured him, her voice less shaky now. 'And I'm certainly pleased to see you. Where are the rest of the rescue team?'

The moonlight was falling directly on to his face, so she clearly saw his dark brows draw together in a brief frown.

'What rescue team?'

'You're not from the hotel?' she questioned him, puzzled. 'Aren't there a lot of people out, looking for me?'

'If there are, I haven't seen any sign of them. I was taking a quiet walk when I suddenly heard you yelling your head off. I thought I was hallucinating,' he added, the hard line of his mouth beginning to relax a fraction. 'The last thing I expected to hear tonight was someone bawling at me from the top of a cliff.'

'If you're not from the hotel, where on earth did you come from?' asked Bethan.

'An archaeological dig. Our camp's in the next valley, about half a mile from here.'

'You're an archaeologist?'

'No, a merchant banker.'

Bethan groaned. 'Let's get this straight. You're a merchant banker, staying at an archaeological dig, who likes to take solitary walks in the Valley of the Kings in the middle of the night?'

'That's about it,' he agreed equably. 'And before this conversation gets any more complicated, perhaps we ought to concentrate on getting you down from this clifftop.'

'That sounds like a very good idea,' Bethan said with some fervour.

'You do realise it was crazy to climb this cliff in the first place?' he said, his voice taking on a severe note. 'The rocks around here are old and crumbling. It's a miracle you didn't fall and break your neck.'

'I've done some climbing before,' she told him defensively. 'I'd never have tackled it if I'd been completely inexperienced. And it wasn't too difficult a climb.'

'Then how come you can't get down again?'

'Because I've wrenched my knee,' came her gloomy answer. 'I got right to the very top, and then this stone just gave way under my foot. My foot slipped, and I twisted my leg as I tried to keep my balance.'

And a scary moment it had been! For several minutes she had just clung there, her heart pounding away as she realised just how close she had come to falling. Then she had somehow hauled herself up the last couple of feet, collapsing in a shaky heap at the top of the cliff. There had been no way she could get down again, though. She couldn't bear to put any weight on her wrenched knee, and it was impossible to climb down without the full use of both legs.

Her rescuer gave a distinctly irritable sigh. 'It's too risky to try carrying you down, especially in the dark. I'll have to return to camp, and get some rope.' When Bethan made a small sound of protest, he glanced down at her with some impatience. 'Can you come up with a better suggestion?'

'No, I suppose not,' she said in a small voice. 'It's just that—well, I don't much like the idea of being left on my own again,' she admitted.

'I won't be long. Probably not more than half an hour.'

'My watch has stopped,' she told him dolefully. 'I haven't got any way I can keep a track of time.'

This time, his sigh was definitely more pronounced. A moment later, he slid off his own watch and transferred it to her slender wrist. The strap was too large, and she had to hold it in place so she could see the luminous dial.

'Quite apart from telling you the time, that watch is a guarantee that I'll be back. It's very expensive!' He glanced down at her. 'Are you cold?'

'Freezing.'

'Then you'd better have this, as well.' He slid off his thick jacket, and handed it to her.

'And is this expensive, too?' Bethan enquired a trifle peevishly, as she wriggled her arms into the soft warmth of the sleeves. 'Have I got to be careful not to get it dirty or rip it?'

His eyes glittered warningly in the moonlight. 'Most people would be very grateful to be rescued from a situation like this. That word doesn't seem to be in your vocabulary, though.'

'I *am* grateful,' she insisted. 'But I'd probably be more grateful if you were just a bit more sympathetic.'

'Only an idiot would have climbed this cliff in the first place. You're in a mess that's entirely of your own making. I prefer to save my sympathy for more deserving causes!' His dark brows drew together in a fierce frown. 'I'd better get back to the camp, to fetch the rope,' he growled, without much enthusiasm. 'Just sit tight until I get back.' Without waiting for her to answer, he made his way to the cliff edge and then swung himself over, carefully searching for, and finding, the first firm footholds. Then he disappeared from sight as he began to climb back down.

'Just sit tight?' Bethan repeated to herself resentfully. What else did he think she was going to do? Sprout a pair of wings and fly away?

Then she frowned. She wasn't behaving very well, and she knew it. Even making allowances for her ordeal of the past few hours, she was still acting like a spoilt brat. Bethan grimaced. The trouble was, that was precisely what she had been for much of her life, and it was hard to shake off old habits. And there was something about this man that just seemed to bring out the worst side of her character. She was thoroughly relieved that he had come charging to her rescue, of course. It was just unfortunate that she had had to be rescued by someone so thoroughly unpleasant.

All the same, she found herself waiting more and more anxiously for his return. She definitely didn't like being on her own. This place was spooky. It would be far too easy to let her imagination run away with her, to start seeing the ghosts of all the old pharaohs flitting around the valley below,

She shivered, snuggled a little deeper into the jacket, and then glanced at the heavy watch on her wrist. It was all right, she assured herself shakily. He would definitely be coming back. He might not be too thrilled about rescuing her, but he would certainly want to get back his watch and his jacket.

The minutes absolutely dragged by, though, and she could feel her nerves stretching nearly to breaking-point. Where was the damned man? Half an hour, he had said, and no it was nearly . . . Bethan checked the watch, then sighed. It was barely thirty minutes since he had left. She could hardly believe it. It seemed more like a couple of hours! Perhaps the watch had stopped? She stared at it, and saw the second hand moving round steadily. No, it was still going. Of course it was, she muttered to herself with edgy sarcasm. An expensive watch like that wouldn't stop, would it?

Then the glimmer of lights in the distance caught her attention. Headlights? Yes! she said to herself with a deep sigh of relief. Definitely headlights.

A couple of minutes later, she could make out the shape of a Land Rover bumping its way to a halt at the foot of the cliff. A familiar tall figure got out, lifted a couple of things out of the back, and then strode towards the cliff-face again.

This time, he climbed more slowly. When he reached the top, Bethan realised why. He was carrying a heavy coil of rope wound round his shoulder. Efficiently, he disengaged himself from the rope and then began to tie it around her, fastening it securely under her arms.

'It'll cut in a little,' he warned, 'but the jacket should help to cushion it.'

When the rope was finally tied to his satisfaction, he made her sit on the edge of the cliff, with her legs dangling over into the void below. Bethan glanced down once, then immediately wished she hadn't. The ground seemed a frighteningly long way away.

'Are you sure you'll be able to hold me?' she asked, suddenly nervous.

He glanced down at her thin body with obvious amusement. 'I think I'll be able to manage it,' he said drily. 'Are you ready?'

Bethan swallowed hard, and then nodded.

'Use your good leg as much as you can to keep yourself steady,' he instructed. 'It'll be bumpy, but there's not much I can do about that. This is the only way I can get you down.'

Seconds later, the rope bit in under her arms as he took her full weight, and she was very glad of the thick jacket. Then he was lowering her, slowly and carefully, loose stones rattling down with her as she rather painfully began the descent.

It seemed to take ages to reach the bottom, but at last there was firm ground under her feet. Bethan began to breathe easily again. Freeing herself from the rope, she hopped awkwardly over to a nearby rock, and then sat and waited for him as he easily climbed down.

He came over to join her, sitting beside her and rubbing his hands together.

'You're not quite as light as you look,' he admitted ruefully.

'Did you hurt your hands?' she asked slightly anxiously.

'The rope burnt some skin off my palms, that's all.' He looked at her. 'At least I'm convinced now that I didn't dream the whole thing. When I came back, I wasn't entirely sure that I'd find you still there. I was beginning to think you must have been a figment of my imagination, that I'd been reading so many books about the old queens of Egypt that I'd somehow conjured one up. Dark hair, dark eyes—you looked just like a ghost of Queen Nefertiti.'

'Except that she was a legendary beauty,' commented Bethan, who had seen photos of Nerfertiti's statue. 'I'm not downright ugly, but I'm certainly not in her league.'

'You look pretty good from here,' he commented casually.

Bethan's eyes suddenly flickered uneasily. She didn't much like the way this conversation was going. After all, what did she actually know about this man? Absolutely nothing! she realised with a fresh rush of edginess. He had said he was a merchant banker, but he could have been lying. He certainly didn't *look* like a merchant banker in those jeans and that loose cotton shirt—although he could hardly be expected to wear a formal business suit in these sort of surroundings, she realised with a small quirk of her eyebrows. All the same, perhaps she had better be rather careful from now on.

'I'm very thirsty,' she said, edging the conversation back on to a safer topic. 'Have you got anything to drink?'

'There's a canteen of water in the Land Rover. I'll carry you over there.'

'No!' she said instantly, a little note of panic creeping back into her voice. 'I can walk to the Land Rover. Well, hop,' she corrected herself hurriedly.

He didn't even bother to argue with her. Instead, he got to his feet and then simply scooped her up, ignoring all her protests.

'You're a very overbearing man!' she told him furiously.

'Am I? Yes, you're probably right,' he agreed, after a short, considering pause.

His cool acceptance of her accusation incensed her even more.

'Do you always throw your weight around like this? If you do, you can't have too many friends.'

'Male? Or female?'

The smug insinuation behind his casual remark made her see red.

'What are you trying to say? That women *like* brute force?'

'Not brute force,' he agreed easily. 'But some of them—quite a lot of them, in fact—seemed to enjoy a little male domination at times.'

Bethan glared at him. 'You are unbelievable! And I certainly don't want to be carried around by a man like you! Put me down, or I'll—I'll——'

But it was impossible to think of any threat that would be effective against this man. Physically strong, completely self-confident, he gave the impression that absolutely nothing would shake him. She couldn't think of a single thing that would make even the slightest impact on him. Giving in to a wave of total frustration, she bit his ear.

He didn't say a single word. He didn't even give a grunt of pain, though she knew she must have hurt him. His lack of response completely unnerved her, especially now her quick surge of anger was subsiding just as quickly as it had flared up.

A few seconds later, they reached the Land Rover. He dumped her on the front seat but, instead of moving away, he loomed over her until his face was only inches away. She couldn't see his features very clearly, but she could most definitely make out the glitter of his eyes and the hard, straight line of his mouth.

'Just this once, I'm willing to make allowances for you,' he said in a voice that was very quiet and very even, and yet still sent shivers rippling down her spine. 'You've obviously been through a rough time today, and it's making you behave like a spoilt and bad-tempered child. But if you ever try anything like that again—you'll soon regret it. Do you understand?'

Bethan nodded jerkily. All the fight had suddenly gone out of her. He was right, it *had* been a rough day, and she certainly wasn't up to coping with a furiously angry male right now. Anyway, what on earth had made her behave like that? All right, so he had provoked her. That was still no excuse for *biting* him! Especially after he had gone to a lot of trouble to rescue her from the predicament she had got herself into. A deep sense of shame rolled over her, and she knew she ought to apologise. Before she could force out the words, though, he had swung himself into the seat beside her.

'Are you still thirsty?' he asked.

'Yes.' Her voice sounded rather sulky, and she was ashamed of that, but couldn't seem to do anything about it. This man just seemed to bring out the most deplorable traits in her character.

He reached into the back of the Land Rover, then handed her a canteen of water. 'Drink it slowly,' he warned. 'Just a few small sips at first.'

She wanted to gulp it straight down, but instead made herself do as he had instructed. After a few mouthfuls, she began to feel better.

'Wait a couple of minutes before you have any more,' he told her. 'Try and drink too much at once, and it'll just make you ill.'

With a small sigh, she set the canteen to one side. 'Perhaps this would be a good time to introduce ourselves,' she suggested.

He shot her a dry glance. 'I feel as if I've already known you for a long time. But if you want to put the whole thing on a formal footing—I'm Maximilian Lansdelle.'

Her eyebrows lifted sky-high. 'That's a bit of a mouthful!'

'Most people shorten it to Max.'

'I'm not surprised. I'm Bethan Lawrence.'

'Well, Bethan Lawrence, I wish I could say it was a pleasure to make your acquaintance. My ear's rather too painful for that, though.'

Instantly, she flushed bright red. 'I'm awfully sorry about that,' she mumbled. 'I don't know why I did it. Yes, I do,' she corrected herself, 'it was because you made me so mad—but that still doesn't excuse it. I've never done anything like that before. At least, not *exactly* like that,' she conceded, reluctantly remembering certain episodes from the past. 'Sometimes I over-react when someone makes me really lose my temper—or makes me feel trapped. Then I do get a bit—physical,' she finished, rather shamefacedly.

'So I've gathered,' he replied with some acerbity. Then, relenting slightly, he added, 'Have some more water.' After she had had another drink, he relaxed back in the seat, half turning so that he was facing her. 'How do you feel now?'

'Not too bad,' she admitted. 'My knee's still pretty painful, but it'll be all right as long as I don't put any weight on it for the next couple of days. I've wrenched it like this before. There's an old weakness there, from an injury I got years ago. I fell out of a tree,' she added, by way of explanation.

One eyebrow lifted expressively. 'You certainly seem to be injury-prone! But since you're feeling better, perhaps it's time you told me exactly what you were doing on top of that cliff.'

Bethan sighed. 'It's a long story.'

'I rather thought it might be.'

'Wouldn't you rather wait until the morning?' she asked hopefully. 'It must be getting very late.'

'It's just gone midnight,' he said, to her surprise. She had been sure it was much later than that.

'You're probably tired,' she argued. 'You've had a fairly hectic evening.'

'I'm fine—so start talking.'

With a sigh, Bethan abandoned the argument. It was obvious he was going to make her sit here until she had told him everything he wanted to know. Then her dark brows drew together slightly as she wondered how much she could reasonably leave out without him suspecting that she wasn't telling the entire truth. It wasn't a pretty story, and she wasn't looking forward to having to go into all the tacky details. Finally, though, she gave a resigned sigh. She had the feeling this man would instantly pick up any lies or omissions—it wasn't worth the hassle. She might as well tell him and get it over with.

'I work for an advertising agency,' she began. 'I don't write brilliant slogans or plan multi-million-pound campaigns,' she added quickly, not wanting him to get the wrong impression. 'I just answer the phone, run messages, look after clients when they arrive for an appointment——'

'In other words, you're window-dressing,' he cut in bluntly. 'You're there because they want someone in the reception area who looks good.'

Bethan supposed she should have been mad at that suggestion. Since it was the truth, though, it wasn't really worth the effort. She certainly hadn't been hired because of her brilliant academic achievements or scintillating career record—neither of which existed! She had been taken on because she was attractive and and knew how to dress. That all helped to create a good impression on clients when they arrived at the agency.

'Yes, I'm window-dressing,' she said stiffly. 'Not that it's any business of yours! Anyway, four of the others who work at the agency were booked on a package holiday to Egypt. One of the girls had to drop out at the last moment, though, so I was asked if I'd like to take her place. I had a couple of weeks' holiday due, and I could just about scrape together the money, so I jumped at the chance. I knew all three of them fairly well—Pauline, Dave and Roger—so I didn't think there'd be any problems.'

Max looked at her quizzically. 'That was rather naïve of you.'

'Yes, it was!' she agreed glumly. 'As soon as we got to Cairo, Pauline and Dave paired off—which left me with Roger.'

'Not the stuff that dreams are made of?'

Bethan grimaced. 'Not *my* dreams! Roger turned out to be pretty thick-skinned, though. He didn't seem to know the meaning of the word "no". He chased me round the pyramids, pestered me all through the bazaars, and then spent half the night tapping on the door of my hotel room. I nearly packed up and went straight back home. Then I made up my mind I wasn't going to let that creep ruin my holiday. We travelled down to Luxor for the second half of the holiday, and this morning, we all set off for a tour of the Valley of the Kings. We went into a couple of the tombs to look at the wall paintings, and you know what it's like inside those tombs, all dark corners and shadowy chambers. Roger waited until I was on my own, and then pounced on me.' She shuddered. 'He was all over me before I realised what was happening. He wasn't exactly subtle, either. He went at it with all the finesse of a great ape!'

'What did you do?' asked Max.

'I kicked him as hard as I could on the shins. And I wished I'd kicked him somewhere even more painful!' Bethan glared at him defiantly. 'I told you, I get rather physical when someone makes me mad.'

Max fingered his ear ruefully. 'I already know that. So what happened after you'd virtually crippled this poor Roger?'

'Poor Roger?' she repeated indignantly. 'I hope he

can't walk properly for a week!' She snorted angrily, then went on, 'After I'd escaped from him, I just bolted. I was so furious, I was practically crying, and I didn't want anyone to see me like that. I headed away from all the crowds of tourists, and then I just kept walking. I don't know how long I kept going, or how far I went, but when I finally stopped and looked around, it dawned on me that I didn't have the slightest idea where I was.'

'It wasn't a very bright thing to do, to rush off like that,' Max commented.

'At the time, I wasn't thinking straight,' Bethan muttered a trifle sulkily, thinking that he could have been just a little more understanding. The whole episode had been a thoroughly unpleasant experience, and he wasn't making the slightest effort to sympathise with her.

'I suppose you got totally lost?' he remarked, his voice actually starting to sound slightly bored now.

'Yes,' she said, hating to admit it. 'I thought I'd be able to find my way back quite easily, but I couldn't. I just seemed to be going round and round in circles. That was when I decided to climb the cliff.'

'And what good did you think that was going to do?'

'I'd have thought that was fairly obvious,' she said, with some indignation. 'I was sure that once I'd got to the top, I'd be able to see a lot further, and then I'd know which way to go.'

'And what did you actually see once you'd reached the top?'

'Only more hills,' she admitted. 'And they all looked exactly the same, brown and bare. And of course, I'd wrenched my knee by then, so I couldn't even get down again.'

'Even if you hadn't wrenched your knee, the whole

idea was completely crazy. What if you'd fallen? Seriously injured yourself?'

Bethan swallowed hard. 'All right, I *know* it was stupid,' she muttered in a low voice. 'Only, at the time, I couldn't think what else to do. And I was stuck at the top of that cliff for hours! I was beginning to think no one was ever going to come and rescue me, that I was going to be there for ever, I was going to d-die there——'

She sniffed miserably, and Max sighed; then he reached into his pocket and handed her a handkerchief. Bethan blew her nose a couple of times, wiped her eyes, and then sat twisting the hankie between her fingers.

Max reached over and switched on the ignition.

'Where are we going?' she asked shakily.

'I'll have to take you back to our camp for the night. In the morning, you can go back to your hotel in Luxor.'

Bethan felt too tired and dispirited to argue with him. Anyway, she didn't really care where she spent the night. She just wanted to curl up somewhere warm and safe, then sleep and sleep. The turmoil of the last few hours was finally catching up with her, and she suddenly felt totally drained of all energy. Her eyes were positively drooping now with wave after wave of exhaustion.

The Land Rover bumped its way across the uneven ground, and only the rough jolting kept her awake. Then it came to a halt again, and in the moonlight she could see a small huddle of tents set in the lee of a high cliff.

'This is it,' said Max. 'Home, sweet home.'

This time, she didn't make any protest when he lifted her out of the Land Rover and carried her over to the nearest tent. Even if both of her legs had been in good working order, she didn't think she could have stood up without help.

It was dark inside the tent, but Max seemed to know exactly where everything was. He set her down on something that felt like a camp bed; then she heard him moving around. A moment later, a dim light illuminated the tent as he lit a small lamp.

He studied her pale face, then frowned. 'You look as if you've just been hit by delayed shock. A drop of brandy will help to pull you round.'

She tried to tell him she didn't want it, but she was beginning to learn that no one won an argument with Maximilian Lansdelle once he had decided on something. The brandy burned its way down her throat, then settled warmly in her stomach. She did feel slightly better afterwards, but she was still just as tired. More so, in fact, because the strong spirit was beginning to work its way into her system, relaxing all her tense muscles.

She pulled off his jacket and handed it back to him. Then she stretched out on the camp bed, gave a huge yawn, and knew she was going to be asleep in just a couple of minutes. Her eyes began to droop shut, but then suddenly flew open again as she felt hands beginning to unbutton her blouse—and those hands definitely weren't hers!

'What——?' she began muzzily, her nerves sending confused warning messages to her over-tired brain.

Max's own eyes—their colour still a mystery—gazed straight back at her.

'Don't read anything into this that isn't there,' he told her, his voice quite relaxed. 'I'm just making you more comfortable, that's all.'

'I'm quite comfortable already,' she muttered stiffly.

He took absolutely no notice. His hands continued unfastening her blouse, deftly slipping the buttons out of the tiny buttonholes in a way that suggested he had done this sort of thing many times before. Probably hundreds, Bethan told herself with a disapproving sniff. She had met men like Maximilian Lansdelle before; experience and expertise just seemed to ooze out of them.

Then his fingers brushed very briefly against one breast as he finally slid the blouse from her shoulders. To her astonishment—and alarm—she had to fight hard to suppress a tiny, involuntary gasp. Had that touch been an accident? Yes, she was sure it had been, because his hands weren't lingering; they were already moving on to quickly and efficiently undo her skirt.

He freed it from her legs; then, before she had fully recovered from that last shock, it happened again. The back of his hand touched her thigh this time, and for a moment she felt as if she had been burnt. It was because she was so tired, she told herself confusedly. Anyway, it obviously hadn't meant anything to him, because he was already drawing a light blanket over her, covering her thinly elegant arms and legs, slender waist and surprisingly full breasts.

She closed her eyes again, and thought he had finally moved away. She didn't realise she was mistaken until his hands returned, to her hair this time, which was still twisted into the thick plait which had kept it out of her eyes while she had climbed the cliff.

With surprising gentleness, he unplaited it, its heavy warmth spilling over his fingers. She hadn't expected to hear him speak again. And when he did, it was little more than a husky murmur under his breath.

'Dark silk,' he muttered, in a low tone that was very different from any she had heard from him so far.

She forced her heavy eyes half-open and found that he was still sitting there, one glossy black strand of her hair wound round his finger, as if he found it surprisingly hard to let it go. She was too exhausted to protest, though. Not that there was any real problem, she told herself sleepily. He had unplaited her hair, that was all, and found he liked the touch and feel of it. A lot of men reacted like that—it didn't really mean anything.

With a small sigh, she shut her eyes for the last time and plummeted straight into a deep, dreamless sleep.

CHAPTER TWO

BETHAN woke up to find herself lying on a narrow camp bed, and staring at a canvas wall. For a few moments, she wrinkled her forehead in perplexed confusion. A tent? What on earth was she doing lying in a tent? And why was her head feeling muzzy and achy, and her skin tingling as if sunburnt?

Then she suddenly sat bolt upright as all the events of yesterday came flooding back into her mind. The revolting episode in the tomb with Roger; her frantic efforts to avoid his groping hands and wet mouth; the hours she had spent stuck up on that cliff, all the time getting more and more frightened. And then, finally, the vivid memory of the man who had rescued her. Max Lansdelle—was this his tent? His bed? She supposed it had to be. But where had he slept?

Somewhere hard and uncomfortable, she hoped. She knew that wasn't a very grateful attitude to take to the man who had most likely saved her life. He certainly didn't go out of his way to make himself liked, though, so she could hardly be blamed for reacting to his abrasive manner.

Rather gingerly, she swung her legs over the side of the bed, and then tested her injured knee. It was still painful and wouldn't take her weight. Bethan sighed. From experience, she knew she would be hopping around for another couple of days.

Her gaze flicked over to her dust-covered skirt and crumpled blouse, which were lying on a small folding chair. Max must have left them there last night, after he had undressed her. Bethan stared at them for a moment, reluctantly remembering that burning sensation as Max's hand had briefly brushed against her. Then she rather impatiently shook her head. It wasn't anything to worry about. Just tiredness and too much brandy, that was all. She might even have imagined the whole thing. She had practically been asleep—perhaps she had actually dropped off, and dreamt it.

She didn't fancy putting those clothes on again, though—they definitely needed a good wash first—so she took the sheet off the camp bed and wound it round her. Then she hopped over to take a look at herself in the shaving mirror that stood on a small table at the far end of the tent.

One look at her reflection made her eyebrows shoot up in dismay. Every part of her skin which had been exposed to the sun yesterday was now glowing bright red. Even Roger would have been put off touching her, she told herself gloomily. Men didn't usually go for women who looked like lobsters!

Hopping back to the camp bed, she sat down again and wondered what she should do now. She was still awfully thirsty; she would have given almost anything for a long, cool drink. The problem was, she could hardly leave the tent wearing just a sheet. All the same, she was seriously considering abandoning her modesty when the flap of the tent was suddenly thrown back and someone came bouncing in.

'Hi,' said a bright, cheerful voice. 'You must be Mr Lansdelle's lost sheep.'

Bethan smiled back at the girl who had flung herself down into the folding chair.

'Yes. I'm Bethan Lawrence.'

'And I'm Poppy,' announced the girl. 'Actually, my name's Georgina, but everyone's called me Poppy since the day I was born—for obvious reasons!'

Bethan's smile broadened. Even in the subdued light inside the tent, Poppy's red hair glowed with almost fluorescent brightness.

'I expect you're thirsty,' went on Poppy. 'I've brought you some fruit juice, but for heaven's sake don't gulp it down too fast or you'll be sick. It's hard, I know, when your tongue must be practically hanging down to the ground, but you must have got rather dehydrated yesterday after being out in the sun all those hours. You've got to keep drinking small amounts at regular intervals for a while.'

'I understand,' nodded Bethan. She slowly drank half the fruit juice, then looked up at Poppy. 'Max—er—Mr Lansdelle told you what happened?'

'Only the very basic facts. He said you'd got lost and he'd found you.' Poppy's gaze drifted over the sheet Bethan had wrapped round herself. 'Do you want to borrow some clothes?' she asked practically.

'Would you mind? I'd be really grateful.'

'They won't be anything fancy,' Poppy warned. 'There's never any opportunity to wear anything except really casual stuff on an archaeological dig. Hang on a sec, and I'll fetch you something.'

She was back in a couple of minutes with a pair of faded cotton jeans and a baggy T-shirt.

'I expect you're dying for a shower,' she said slightly apologetically, 'but the only water we've got at the camp is what we bring in ourselves. Life's pretty primitive at a dig like this, although you soon get used to it when you're actually working here.'

Bethan gave a philosophical shrug, and pulled on the clothes Poppy had brought her. Then she sat down again on the camp bed, to take the weight off her injured knee, and began to drag a comb through her tangled hair.

'What are you looking for at this dig?' she asked Poppy. 'Old jars and pots, things like that?'

'I'm not sure,' admitted Poppy. 'Peter Wallace—he's in charge of the dig—just marks out squares on the ground and then says, "Dig there!" As far as I can make out, we're just doing some preliminary surveys at the moment. I think he's hoping we'll eventually turn up something interesting, so he'll know the right spot to start a more detailed excavation.'

'And where does Max Lansdelle fit into all this?'

'He's an old friend of Peter's—I think they were at university together. When Peter was short of finance to get the excavation under way, Mr Lansdelle stepped in and provided the extra money he needed.'

Bethan shook her head. 'I didn't mean that. I meant, what's he doing *here*? He doesn't strike me as the type to muck in with the digging and get his hands dirty.'

'He had to come to Egypt on business,' explained Poppy,' so he decided to come down to the dig for a few days, to see how things were going.' Then she grinned. 'To be honest, I don't really care why he's here. I just like having him around. Not that I'm getting anywhere,' she added, with a rueful shrug. 'It looks as if he doesn't go for redheads.'

Bethan looked at her in surprise. 'You're interested in him?'

'All that charm and good looks—and money? You bet I'm interested. I'm not holding out much hope, though. Apart from anything else, there's a fiancée lurking somewhere in the background. If some woman's been lucky enough to get her claws into Max

Lansdelle, you can bet she isn't going to let go without a fight.'

'How do you know all this?' asked Bethan, fascinated.

'Steve—he's the other student on the dig—knows the fiancée. She's a friend of his older sister. He's even met her a couple of times.' Poppy pulled a face. 'Steve says she's one of those ice-cool blondes, stunning to look at, sickeningly elegant, a real head-turner. If you've got any designs on Mr Lansdelle, I think you'd better forget them. The competition's too fierce for you and me, kiddo.

Bethan sniffed. 'As far as I'm concerned, she's welcome to him. I wouldn't want him even if he came gift-wrapped.'

'Well, I certainly would,' declared Poppy without hesitation. 'And if I were his fiancée, I wouldn't let him out of my sight for a single second. Still, I suppose it means she feels pretty sure of him, letting him go gallivanting off round the world without her.'

Poppy's voice quickly trailed away as a familiar tall figure appeared in the doorway of the tent, blocking out most of the sun. Bethan clearly heard Poppy's audible gulp and nervously wondered, like the other girl, just how much of their conversation Max Lansdelle had overheard.

'I—er—I think I'd better get back to the dig,' mumbled Poppy, very hurriedly backing out of the tent. 'I've got a lot of work to get on with——'

After she had made her escape, Max came right into the tent and seated himself on the folding chair. The sunlight was streaming in through the open tent flaps and falling full on to his face, so Bethan had a chance to see him clearly for the first time.

She had known his hair was dark, but she hadn't

realised that it was almost as black as her own. His skin was deeply tanned, as if he had spent a lot of time out in the sun during the past few days—and he probably tanned quickly and easily, she thought to herself with a quick burst of resentment. He wouldn't glow like a lobster after a few hours in the sun!

Then her gaze slid down to his hands. They were strong and long-fingered, and she wondered if the rope burns on his palms were less painful this morning. Perhaps she should ask him, it would be only polite. Just then, though, he raised his head, letting her see his eyes.

Last night, there hadn't been enough light to reveal their true colour, but she had guessed they were dark, to match his hair. She had been wrong, though. Instead, they were a glowing amber—like a hunting animal's, she told herself edgily. If it hadn't been for those eyes, she might have thought he was a cool customer. They gave him away, though. She wondered if he realised just how much they revealed. If he had, he might have kept them shuttered, so she couldn't read the message in them quite so easily.

Hungry eyes. The eyes of a man with a strong sexual appetite, which he was used to gratifying without too much trouble. Bethan shivered. There couldn't be too many opportunities for finding an outlet for those powerful needs at an archaeological dig. Was she heading straight into deep trouble?

When Max spoke, though, his voice was quite calm and he seemed perfectly relaxed. 'Did you sleep well last night?'

It was a few moments before Bethan answered. Inside her, something was still gently quivering.

'Yes, thanks,' she managed to get out at last.

'And does your knee feel any better this morning?'

Realising with some relief that there weren't going to be any problems, that this man had more than enough self-control to cope with his own frustration, Bethan gradually became less tense.

'I told you last night, it'll be a couple more days before I can put any weight on it. Apart from that, though, I'm fine.'

'Then you'd better tell me the name of your hotel in Luxor,' Max said. 'I'll get a message to them, letting them know you're safe and well, and that you'll be back some time later today.'

'Er—there might be some difficulty there,' Bethan ventured cautiously.

Max instantly began to look displeased. 'What kind of difficulty?'

'You know I was on a package tour? Everyone was due to leave today on a Nile cruise, from Luxor to Aswan. They'll have left by now. And since the whole party will have been booked out from the hotel, my room will have been allocated to someone else.'

His amber eyes registered a fresh glow of impatience. Max Lansdelle was obviously a man who didn't like to have his plans thwarted in any way.

'Miss Lawrence——' he began.

Oh, I see! she thought to herself, instinctively straightening her shoulders as if bracing herself for a fight. So we're going to be very formal this morning, are we?

'Miss Lawrence, I don't see that should cause any major problems. If you get in touch with the local courier, I'm sure she'll arrange for you to join the cruise ship a little further along the Nile.'

'Mr Lansdelle,' replied Bethan, deliberately answering him in the same formal tone, 'there's one rather important point that you've overlooked. I've decided that I don't *want* to rejoin that package tour.'

Her blunt statement went down about as well as a plate of cold porridge. Max's mouth set into a straight line, and his dark brows drew together.

'Look,' she went on placatingly, 'it's been bad enough trying to get away from Roger these last few days. Imagine what it's going to be like if I'm stuck on a cruise ship with him. I'll never get a minute's peace!'

'Are you sure you're not over-estimating your attractions?' he drawled, the veiled insult making her hackles rise.

'You weren't around when that creep jumped on me yesterday,' she flashed back furiously. 'It was practically—well, practically attempted rape!'

If she had been expecting instant concern, then it was obvious she was going to be disappointed. Max didn't bat an eyelid. In fact, he merely looked sceptical. Bethan scowled. Perhaps that *had* been a bit over the top; Roger had gone in for some heavy groping, but not much more. Nevertheless, she thought she deserved a lot more sympathy that she was getting.

'I don't see that you've got any alternative except to rejoin that package tour,' Max told her evenly. 'Unless, of course, you're planning to return straight home to England.'

'But I've still got over a week of my holiday left,' she pointed out.

'Then perhaps the hotel in Luxor will let you stay for a few more days. Although I wouldn't count on it, this is one of their busiest times of the year. Vacant rooms are fairly thin on the ground.'

An idea suddenly came into Bethan's head. Without even thinking about it, she blurted out, 'I suppose I couldn't stay here?'

Max looked at her as if she had just made a very bad joke. 'No,' he said, an instant later. He didn't add anything else, but he didn't need to. That one word had been totally final.

Bethan gave a rather sulky shake of her head. What an unreasonable man he was!

'You still haven't told me the name of your hotel,' Max reminded her, a few moments later. He handed her a piece of paper and a pen. 'Scribble it down, and I'll send a message to say you'll be arriving some time this afternoon.'

Reluctantly, she wrote it down, and then handed the piece of paper back to him.

'I'll get Poppy to bring you a light lunch,' he went on. 'As soon as you've eaten, Ahmed will drive you to the ferry that crosses over the Luxor. Goodbye, Miss Lawrence.'

And that was it? she thought, blinking. Apparently it was, because he got up and left the tent without saying another word. Not exactly the sociable type, she muttered to herself crossly. And not very friendly, either. All he seemed to want to do was to get rid of her as quickly as he could.

She wasn't at all sure that she wanted to go, though. Oh, not because of Max Lansdelle, she assured herself hurriedly. He was most definitely *not* the reason why she had decided she wanted to stay right here. It was just that she didn't want to go back home yet—Egypt was turning out to be a fascinating country, and she was eager to learn more about its colourful past and its ancient civilisations. And what better place to do that than an archaeological dig? Anyway, what would she be going back to in England? A lonely bedsit and a boring job. She wrinkled her nose. Two very good reasons for *not* going back. And she had never been involved in an archaeological dig before; it was bound to be interesting.

Poppy came trotting over about half an hour later, carrying a small tray.

'Lunch,' she announced. 'It's not very exciting,' she added, rather apologetically. 'Practically everything comes out of tins, and it's just a question of whether you eat it hot or cold. Today it's kind of tepid,' she said with a grimace. 'I'm not the world's greatest cook. In fact, I might even be the worst.'

Bethan looked at the plate of tinned meat and vegetables, and somehow managed an enthusiastic smile. 'Thanks, it looks—er—fine.'

'No, it doesn't,' Poppy said truthfully. 'It looks atrocious. Don't eat it if you don't want to. I won't be offended.'

'I'm so hungry, I could eat just about anything—even your cooking,' Bethan said with a grin.

'Can't stop, I'm afraid. We've just started excavating a new site, and Peter's got everyone working flat out. See you later.'

Bethan ate quickly, ignoring the bland taste of the food; then she pushed the tray to one side and ran her fingers through her slightly damp hair. Even with the flaps open, the interior of the tent was getting overwhelmingly hot and stifling. The main problem with this country was the temperature, she grumbled softly to herself. It was far too hot during the day, and chillingly cold at night. All extremes, no nice happy medium.

She levered herself to her feet, and moved the folding chair to the entrance of the tent, where the air was fractionally fresher and cooler. Then, while she drank the glass of fruit juice that Poppy had brought with her meal, she surveyed her surroundings.

The camp site was situated in a narrow valley that was surrounded by the familiar dusty brown hills. No matter which way she looked, it was bleak and barren, with no trace of greenery anywhere. Yet the shifting shadows as the sun crept across the sky, the stark colours and the shimmering heat haze that slightly blurred everything, gave it a strange sort of beauty.

She finished the juice, and then wriggled slightly uncomfortably. Somewhere around here, there had to be some sort of bathroom facilities, even though they would probably turn out to be fairly primitive. Bethan looked around. There were several tents, all pitched in the lee of the high cliff behind them. One of them probably contained a chemical toilet or some similar arrangement. The only problem was, which one was it?

She hauled herself out of the chair; then she hopped awkwardly over to the nearest tent and peered inside. Obviously not this one, she told herself ruefully. It was very similar to the tent she had just left, containing a camp bed and a few other essential items. Doggedly, she hopped on to the next one, which was a little further away, and was just about to look inside when she heard the murmur of voices.

She hurriedly backed away, and was about to move on when she heard a voice she didn't recognise, the words sounding perfectly clear through the thin canvas walls.

'I still think it was a mistake bringing her here, Max. We don't even know who she really is. What if she's some damned reporter, and that story about being lost was just a ruse to trick her way in here?'

Max's distinctive voice immediately answered, his tone calm and relaxed.

'No one, not even a reporter, is going to go to those

sort of lengths to get a story. The girl was genuinely stuck on the top of that cliff, Peter. She might even have died if I hadn't found her and brought her down.'

Bethan's ears instantly pricked up. Peter? Then it must be Peter Wallace whom Max was talking to, the man who had organised this excavation. But why was he getting so worked up over her being here? Why was he worried in case she was a reporter?

Max was talking again. 'She's just a silly young girl who ran off after some tiff with a boyfriend, and then got lost. It was pure coincidence I found her and brought her here. There's no way she could have found out anything of any importance. Not even Poppy and Steve know the real reason why we're here. You and I are the only two who know what you're really looking for at this excavation.'

By now, Bethan's ears were positively flapping. What were they talking about? Something very important, obviously. And something that might prove very useful, if she could only find out a bit more about it.

Eavesdropping quite shamelessly, she edged slightly nearer to the tent, balancing precariously on one leg like a wobbly stork.

She heard Peter Wallace give a deep sigh. 'We've done a fair amount of digging, and so far we've discovered nothing. I'd hoped we'd come across something long before now.'

'You're sure this is the right place?' Max's voice was cool and unruffled, in sharp contrast to Peter's worried tones.

'You can never be absolutely sure about something like this. All the years of research I've done point to it, though. More than that, though, I've got a gut feeling that tells me it's right here. We might even be sitting right on top of it. Only now this wretched girl's turned up,' Peter reminded him with a fresh burst of worried irritation. 'And just as we've started excavating the new site. It couldn't have happened at a more inconvenient time.'

'She'll be no problem,' Max assured him smoothly. 'I've arranged for her return to Luxor this afternoon.'

'Good.' The relief in Peter's voice was very obvious. 'We've got to do everything we can to stop any rumours spreading. If word starts to buzz around the bazaars and villages of what we're really looking for, every petty thief between Cairo and Aswan will start swarming all over the site. And if that happens, we might as well just pack up and go home.'

'The girl knows nothing,' came Max's confident assessment. 'She hasn't even left the tent since she's been here.'

Bethan gave a silent snort. That's what he thought! Then her brain began to work overtime, fitting together all the snippets of conversation she had overheard. It was pretty obvious that there was something they didn't want her to find out—but by putting together all the vague hints and by using a little common sense, she already had a good idea what it might be. She wasn't sure that she believed it—the whole thing seemed rather too incredible—but if it *was* true, then she could certainly understand why they didn't want anyone to know about it!

Quivering slightly with excitement, she leant forward, inching a fraction closer to the tent. With luck, she might overhear something that would confirm she was definitely on the right track.

Then, without any warning, a spasm of cramp gripped her strained leg muscles. To her horror, she began to wobble. She flailed her arms wildly, trying to

regain her balance, but it was no good. A couple of
seconds later, she overbalanced completely and went
crashing into the side of the tent.

The canvas collapsed under her weight, and she
heard the muffled sound of someone swearing as
several things in the tent noisily fell over. Then strong
arms were plucking her out of the wreckage and setting
her back on her feet again. Apprehensively, she looked
up and found Max's furious amber gaze staring
straight back at her.

'Er—I was—looking for the bathroom——' she
stuttered feebly.

'And of course, you weren't eavesdropping,' came
his coldly sarcastic reply.

'Definitely not,' she lied brazenly. 'I realised this
was the wrong tent, and I was moving away when
I—well, lost my balance——'

'And how long were you standing outside before
you decided this was the wrong tent?' he enquired, his
tone still freezing.

'Oh, no time at all,' Bethan assured him hurriedly,
not at all liking the expression that had settled over
those fierce eyes. 'A few seconds—perhaps not even
that.'

Max studied her silently for what seemed like hours,
even though it couldn't have been more than a minute
or so. There seemed enough power behind that gaze to
see right through her, and Bethan felt she might shrivel
up completely if he kept it up much longer.

At last, though, to her utter relief, he looked away
from her. 'The tent you're looking for is over there.'
He pointed to one which stood a little apart from the
rest. 'I'll take you.'

'That's not necessary,' she squeaked nervously, but
it was too late. He had already swung her up into

his arms.

'I wouldn't want you to have any more "accidents",' he told her in a voice that was silky smooth now, and yet still made her insides tremble.

In a few strides, they reached the other tent. For one awful moment, Bethan thought he was going to take her right inside. Instead, though, he set her down outside. Then he just stood there and looked at her again until she began to blush bright red. It was a good thing she was so sunburnt, she told herself. With luck, he wouldn't be able to see the added colour flooding her skin.

'When you're ready, I think we've got some talking to do, don't you?' he said meaningfully. And with that rather ominous remark, he left her to hop inside the tent with both her good and her bad leg shaking quite badly.

The sanitary arrangements were basic, but spotlessly clean. Putting off the moment when she would have to come face to face with Max again, she stayed inside for as long as she dared. Finally, though, she had to leave her safe refuge. She peered out, then heaved a sigh of relief when she saw there was no sign of Max. Hoping she would be able to make it back to her own tent without being seen, she began to hop quickly in that direction. She was only half-way there, though, when she let out a soft groan. Max had just come out of one of the other tents, and was already striding purposefully in her direction.

Without a word, he picked her up again and carried her the rest of the way to the tent. He set her down in the chair in the doorway; then he just stood there, looming over her and staring down at her.

'I wish you wouldn't do that,' she muttered.

'Do what?'

'Tower over me like that!'

He seated himself, cross-legged, on the sand beside her. 'Better?' he enquired, a little mockingly.

As a matter of fact, it wasn't, although she didn't intend to tell him that. Whether he was standing, sitting or lying, it didn't seem to make the slightest difference. He could still make her feel totally on edge, and she didn't like that; she didn't like it at all.

'What did you want to say to me?' she asked cagily.

'First of all, that I think you're a liar,' came his cool response. Before she had time to splutter a protest, he went on, 'I think you were standing outside that tent for far longer than you admitted, and that you overheard things you were never meant to hear.' Bethan glared at him furiously, but didn't try to deny it a second time. 'Let's get one thing straight,' Max told her, and this time his tone was edged with pure ice. 'If you repeat one word of it to anyone else—just one word—you'll be in serious trouble. I'll make sure of that. And you'd better believe I've got the influence to ensure this isn't just an empty threat.'

She believed him. Power surrounded this man like an invisible cloud. He would never make any threat he couldn't carry through.

'I didn't hear anything that made any sense,' she mumbled.

'Perhaps not,' Max agreed. 'But maybe you're a lot brighter than you're letting on. You might just put two and two together, and come up with the right answer.'

'I've never been much good at sums.'

'Don't be flippant about this, Bethan,' he warned sharply. 'Just remember what I've said—make sure you keep your mouth shut once you're back in Luxor.'

'Back in Luxor?' she repeated, without much enthusiasm.

Max got to his feet. 'You'll be leaving in about an hour. Ahmed will make sure you get safely back to your hotel.'

Without so much as a goodbye, he wheeled round and strode off. Bethan glared after him. No one ordered her about like that! So, Max Lansdelle thought he had the upper hand? Well, they would see about that!

Yet it was difficult to stay angry for long; for one thing, it was far too hot. The heat of the sun finally lulled her into a light doze, and she didn't wake up again until she heard a soft voice saying her name.

She opened her eyes to find a tall, dark-skinned man standing in front of her.

'I am Ahmed,' he said. 'I have come to take you to Luxor.'

'Hello, Ahmed,' Bethan greeted him. 'I'm afraid there's been a change of plan. I'm not going.'

Ahmed gave a slightly puzzled frown. 'But I was told it had all been arranged——' he began.

'Well, I unarranged it.' Then, seeing he didn't understand her ungrammatical English, she added quickly, 'Mr Lansdelle wants me to go to Luxor. I don't want to go, though, so I'm staying right here.'

Ahmed looked faintly astonished that anyone should even think of disobeying Max Lansdelle's orders. He didn't argue with her, though. Instead, he gave a slightly fatalistic shrug of his shoulders. 'Inshallah,' he murmured, and then walked away.

Inshallah—it was a phrase Bethan had heard more than once since her arrival in Egypt. 'As God wills it.' Only this was more a case of 'as Max Lansdelle wills it', she told herself slightly grimly. Athough Peter Wallace seemed to be theoretically in charge, she wouldn't mind betting that it was Max who, more often than not, had the last word on everything around here.

With a fresh twinge of nervousness, she noted that Ahmed hadn't returned direct to the excavation site, but had instead gone to one of the other tents first. Reporting back to the boss, she concluded with a grimace. Edgily, she waited for Max's next move.

It wasn't a long wait. His tall figure left the tent only a couple of minute later, and then strode rapidly towards her. As he drew nearer, she could see his amber eyes had darkened considerably, and sheer anger was evident in every taut line of his body.

He didn't say a single word. Instead, he grabbed hold of her arm and hauled her to her feet. Then he propelled her into the tent, forcing her to hop awkwardly on her one good leg, but at the same time gripping her so hard that there was no chance of her falling over.

Once they were inside, he flung the flaps shut behind him.

'Right,' he grated in a furious voice. 'Now you can tell me what the hell you're up to!'

CHAPTER THREE

BETHAN didn't answer him straight away. Instead, she collapsed on to the camp bed and then glared up at him resentfully.

'Bully! Is this how you get your kicks? By throwing your weight around?'

Max's expression instantly altered. Now, his eyes glowed with a dangerous light which she had never seen before. One hand snaked out, and a second later she found a strand of her black hair twisted round his finger. He tugged it lightly but not painfully—just enough to let her know that she was pretty helpless at the moment. Then he released her hair and let that same finger run right down the length of her neck, making her shiver involuntarily. His hand paused briefly at the delicate skin at the base of her throat. Then he finally let go of her, took a step back and stared down at her.

'If you like,' he purred challengingly, 'I'll show you exactly how I get my kicks.'

Her skin still seemed to be burning from that light but lethal touch. Bethan scowled up at him, completely on the defensive now.

'I'm really not interested in your sexual party tricks! I'm sure a lot of women think they're absolutely irresistible,' she went on scathingly, 'but I'm definitely not one of them.'

His gaze glinted briefly. Then he seemed to realise things were getting out of hand. Quite deliberately, he shut down all his emotions. His eyes went blank and his face became quite unreadable.

'I don't know how we got side-tracked like this, but I'm certainly not interested in taking it any further,' he informed her very coolly. 'All I want to know right now is why you're being so damned difficult.'

'I don't think I'm being difficult at all,' she retorted. 'You're trying to force me to do something I don't want to do. I've already told you that I don't want to go back to Luxor.'

Irritation flared across his face again. 'But you're not being given any choice. And since you haven't got any luggage, we can leave right now. I'm taking you myself,' he added warningly.

This was the moment Bethan had been steeling herself for, when she would openly have to defy him. Now that it had actually arrived, though, she felt a cowardly urge to spinelessly obey him, to hop into the Land Rover and let him drive her to the ferry that would take her back across the Nile, to Luxor. Don't be so gutless! she lectured herself severely. She lifted her head, tossed back her hair and then faced him squarely.

'What I'd really like to do is stay here and help with the excavation.'

'With one leg out of action?' said Max dismissively. 'You'd be totally useless. Apart from that, you know absolutely nothing about archaeology.'

'My leg will be much better in a couple of days. As for knowing nothing about archaeology—well, there can't be anything too difficult about sifting through a lot of sand.'

But he wasn't even listening any longer; he had already turned away and was moving towards the entrance to the tent. 'I'll fetch the Land Rover,' he

stated, his tone clearly telling her that there wasn't
going to be any further discussion on the subject.

Bethan drew in a deep breath. She wasn't ready to
give up on this yet. She had had time to think about it,
and she knew now what she wanted to do. And she
was sure she could be every bit as stubborn as Max
Lansdelle when it came down to it.

'I'm really grateful for the way you rescued me last
night,' she told him, 'and I realise that puts me in your
debt. But that doesn't give you the right to order me
around.'

Max swung back to face her. 'You want to argue
about rights? What about our right to kick you straight
out of here, because you're not wanted?'

Her mouth set in a determined line. 'I'd have
thought you would have preferred to have me around,
so you could keep an eye on me—to make sure that I
don't say anything I shouldn't,' she added meaningfully.

When she saw the abrupt change in Max's expression, her knees began to shake, but she stood her
ground.

'Would you like to explain that in a little more
detail?' he invited softly.

Bethan shrugged. 'You know what women are like.
We're such chatterboxes—we can't keep quiet about
anything.'

'And you think you know some secret that's worth
telling?'

The quiet menace in his voice almost made her lose
her nerve, but then she told herself there wasn't anything he could actually *do* to her. He might be
absolutely livid, but she thought—she hoped!—that he
wouldn't go as far as physical violence.

'It wasn't too difficult to put all the pieces together,'

she said, hoping she sounded far more confident than
she felt. 'When you and Peter went on and on about
keeping your reason for being here a secret, and being
worried about thieves moving in, it all sort of fell into
place. After all, what's the most exciting thing you can
find in Egypt? The one thing every archaeologist
dreams of discovering? It's fairly obvious, really.'

'Then why don't you tell me what it is?' Max
invited, his face quite expressionless now.

'The lost tomb of one of the Pharaohs, of course,'
she said with growing certainty. 'That's it, isn't it?
What you're really looking for?'

His gaze never left her face. 'I was right,' he said at
last. 'You *are* brighter than you let on.'

'I can understand why you don't want anyone to
know about it,' she rushed on, getting excited now she
knew she had guessed right. 'At least, not until you've
actually found it. A lost tomb,' she repeated softly,
almost to herself. 'Fantastic! I suppose there'll be
treasure, and all sorts of marvellous finds.' Her eyes
began to glow. 'You can understand why I want to
stick around,' she said to Max. 'I wouldn't miss it for
anything.'

'If I'd known you were going to be such a nuisance,
I'd have left you stuck on the top of that cliff,' he
growled.

'But I'm right, aren't I?' she persisted. 'You really
are looking for a lost tomb?'

He gave an irritable but resigned shrug. 'I suppose
there's not much point in trying to deny it.'

'And you'll let me stay?'

Max frowned darkly. 'Have I got any choice? If I
send you back to Luxor, I suppose you'll start blabbing about it to just about everyone you meet.'

'You won't regret it,' Bethan assured him. 'I'll be

useful, honestly I will.'

He didn't look in the least convinced. Nor did he look particularly thrilled at the prospect of having her around for the next few days.

'I'm sorry I had to more or less blackmail you into letting me stay,' she went on apologetically. 'I couldn't see any other way of persuading you, though. And once I'd worked out you were looking for a tomb, I was determined to stick around.'

'And do you always get what you want?'

His terse question, coupled with the deep note of disapproval in his voice, made her glance at him sharply. Who was he to censure her? Then she relaxed again. She was pretty pleased with life at the moment; she didn't intend to spoil things by getting involved in an argument.

'I've been a spoilt brat for most of my life,' she admitted cheerfully. 'Whenever I've wanted something, I've usually got it.'

'And what if we all behaved like that?'

It suddenly dawned on her that he was moving very much closer. He was uncomfortably near now, and it seemed to Bethan that the tent was somehow shrinking, bringing the two of them even closer. She blinked her eyes. It was an optical illusion, she told herself a little shakily. Either that, or the heat was making her feel slightly woozy.

'What—what do you mean?' she asked, feeling the first pricklings of apprehension.

'What if we all just took what we wanted? Or do you think we've got a perfect right to do that?'

'Well, I don't know——' she floundered.

His amber gazed fixed on her. 'If *you* can have what you want, why shouldn't everyone else? For example, if I want *this*,' he went on, 'why shouldn't I have it?'

And without giving her any warning as to what he intended doing, he bent his head and very thoroughly kissed her.

Bethan had been kissed before, but it slowly dawned on her that it had never been quite like this. Privately, she had often thought that it was an over-rated activity, and it usually marked the start of an undignified struggle to stop it going any further. Much more of this, though, she muttered to herself dazedly, and she could well start to change her mind!

Max's kiss was very slow, very pleasurable, and very expert. If he wanted more—and she thought he probably did—then he didn't show it. He explored with his lips, with his tongue, but nothing more. He wasn't even touching her, except to lightly hold her steady with one hand as he continued that long, leisurely exploration of her mouth.

Then it came to an end, as swiftly as it had started. He moved back a fraction, and then gazed down at her, his gaze cool and controlled.

'Because I wanted that kiss, did it mean I had the right to take it?' he challenged her.

'No!' she shot back instantly. Confusion was making her sound more angry than she actually was.

'Yet you seem to think *you've* got the right to do whatever you want,' Max reminded her. 'To barge in here, and demand that we let you stay.'

'That's different.'

'How?'

'It—it just is! Oh, stop lecturing me,' she added a little sulkily.

She knew she was beginning to sound childish, but she couldn't help it. Her brain wouldn't work properly at the moment; she just didn't seem capable of putting up a reasonable argument. What had the man done to her? she wondered irritably. Then she gave a grimace. That was easy enough to answer—he had kissed her! But why on earth had one silly little kiss put her head into this total spin?

To her relief, Max was moving away from her now. Once there was a safe distance between them, she began to feel slightly more in control.

'Peter Wallace isn't going to be very pleased when he finds out I'm staying, is he?' she predicted.

'That's something of an understatement,' Max said curtly. 'Perhaps I'd better go and break the news to him.'

'Will he want to see me?'

'I shouldn't think so. If I were you, I'd stay out of everyone's way for as long as possible. Show your face too soon, and someone might give in to the temptation to try and shake some sense into you!'

And with that last caustic comment, he turned and left the tent.

After he had gone, Bethan sat and brooded over what had happened. Had she behaved very badly? She supposed she had, but there really hadn't been any other alternative. And was she crazy to want to stay? Probably, she decided with a rueful grin. She couldn't let an opportunity like this slip away from her, though. Her life was fairly dull at the moment; she was stuck in a boring job, and her holiday had turned out to be a disaster. At least this promised to be *exciting*.

Perhaps a little too exciting? she wondered with a brief grimace, as she remembered Max's kiss. Then she shook her head. It was all right, it hadn't actually meant anything. Max Lansdelle had a beautiful blonde fiancée waiting for him at home. He wasn't interested in Bethan Lawrence. That kiss had been to teach her a lesson, that was all.

Max returned again in the middle of the afternoon.

'What did Peter Wallace say?' Bethan asked, looking up at him a little apprehensively.

'He wasn't exactly overjoyed at the prospect of having you around.' Max told her. 'In the end, though, I persuaded him that he didn't really have any choice. The alternative was to kick you out, and let you go blabbing to everyone that we were looking for a lost tomb.' His amber gaze rested on her assessingly. 'You do appreciate the need for absolute secrecy, don't you? If word of what Peter's really looking for gets out, we'll not only be over-run with sensation-seeking reporters, but every thief in the district will be homing in on us, waiting for us to find the tomb so they can try to snatch any precious contents from under our noses. Tomb-robbing is regarded as a perfectly legitimate occupation round here. They've been doing it for centuries, and they're absolute experts at it.'

Bethan shook her head in amazement. 'You don't trust anyone, do you? You haven't even told Poppy and Steve what you're really looking for, and they're actually working on the excavation!'

'That isn't because we don't trust them. It's just that it's so easy to be careless, and let a casual word slip in the wrong place. Remember, that's how *you* found out, by overhearing snatches of a private conversation.' Bethan flushed brightly, rather embarrassd by the memories of her blatant eavesdropping. 'The fewer people who know about this, the better,' Max finished.

'I won't tell a soul, I promise I won't,' Bethan assured him. 'And I'll try to be useful while I'm here. Once my knee's better, perhaps I could take over the cooking? That lunch Poppy made me was pretty awful,' she said candidly.

'Poppy's a far better archaeology student than she is a cook,' Max admitted. 'Do you think you can do better?'

'I'm sure I can.'

'All right, you can give it a try. The cooking equipment is set up in a tent at the far end of the camp, and the smaller tent next to it contains all the supplies. If there's anything else you want, tell Ahmed. He makes the trip to Luxor two or three times a week, to fetch whatever we need. Now, about sleeping arrangements—I suppose you'd better move in with Poppy. I'll get Ahmed to put up a camp bed in there for you.'

Bethan leaned forwards eagerly. 'Now you've got the domestic arrangements all fixed up, tell me more about this tomb Peter Wallace is looking for.'

'The first thing you've got to realise is that there's a good chance we'll find nothing at all,' Max warned. 'Just take a look around, and you'll soon see what we're up against. We're looking for a tomb entrance that's probably only six or seven feet wide, and maybe ten feet high. It'll certainly be buried by sand, and perhaps even by a heavy rockfall. We could dig all year in this little valley alone, and never find it. And there are a dozen similar small valleys just beyond the next ridge of hills.'

'Oh,' muttered Bethan, distinctly deflated.

Max raised one eyebrow in dry amusement. 'Did you think it was just a question of poking around in the sand for a couple of days until we found it?'

'I suppose I did,' she confessed, feeling like an absolute half-wit.

'On the other hand,' Max went on, 'Peter's been researching this project for years. He's as sure as he can be that we're in the right spot. So, perhaps we'll just get lucky—that's how most of the great finds are made, in the end. Someone just stumbles across the right spot at the right moment.' He got up. 'But remember what I've said about the need for secrecy,' he warned. 'If word of this ever gets out—Peter and I will know who's responsible.'

Bethan pulled a face at his retreating back as he left the tent, but even Max's repressive remarks couldn't keep her spirits down for long. They were going to let her stay! And whatever the next week or so held in store, she was absolutely positive life wasn't going to be dull.

During the next couple of days, she battled with, and finally got the better of, the temperamental cooking stove. She could put her bad leg to the ground now, hobbling round faster and faster as her knee rapidly improved. Her sunburn was fading from fiery red to a rather nice light bronze, and she sent up a small prayer of thanks that her skin hadn't peeled.

She soon found that she liked Peter Wallace. He was an odd character, often very down to earth, but with bright flashes of romanticism which came through most strongly when he was talking about this land, whose ancient mysteries he was trying to unravel. Steve turned out to be a rather shy young man who was totally absorbed in his work most of the time, and as for Poppy—well, it was impossible not to get on with the cheerful, outgoing Poppy. Bethan *was* getting a bit tired of wearing Poppy's clothes, though. They were a couple of sizes too big for her, and she was forever hitching up the trousers, and having to be careful when she bent down because the borrowed blouse gaped open at the front.

At lunch time the next day, she tentatively

mentioned that it would be rather nice to have her own clothes back again.

Max glanced up. 'What's wrong with those you've got on?'

'They don't fit!' she said in exasperation. If the man opened his eyes and looked at her, he would see she looked like a walking jumble sale.

'It's better to wear loose clothes in this heat,' Max told her, his voice clearly indicating a total lack of interest in the subject.

'I'd still like to wear something that's mine,' she persisted stubbornly. 'Look, next time Ahmed goes to Luxor to get fresh supplies, can't he pick up my luggage from the hotel?'

'I suppose so,' shrugged Max. He turned to Peter. 'How are things going?'

'Not too well,' said Peter gloomily. 'We don't seem to be getting anywhere with this new site we're excavating. If we don't turn up anything in the next couple of days, I might move over to the other side of the valley and try a couple of exploratory excavations there.'

Bethan could hear the disappointment in his voice, and knew he was feeling depressed. Obviously, they were still a very long way from uncovering any new tomb, and she wondered what would happen if they still kept drawing blanks wherever they dug. Now that the initial thrill of being here had worn off, she was feeling a little low herself. Somehow, she had thought it would be more exciting than this. Life at the dig was turning out to be actually rather humdrum.

Ahmed was despatched to Luxor the next day, armed with a long shopping list from Bethan, and in-structions to collect her luggage. It was early evening when he finally returned. They had just begun their main meal of the day, eating out in the open so they could marvel at the unrivalled splendour of an Egyptian sunset at the same time. Every evening it was different, and yet just as magnificent, the radiant sky splashed with the most unbelievably vivid colours.

Going over to Max, Ahmed began to talk to him in a low voice. Max frowned briefly, then gave a resigned shrug. Finally, he turned his head and looked at Bethan.'

'It looks as if you'll be wearing Poppy's cast-offs for a while longer. Your luggage has been sent to Aswan. Apparently, the hotel in Luxor thought it had been left behind by accident after your holiday tour departed, so they forwarded it on.'

Bethan groaned. 'Isn't there any way I can get it back again?'

'I'm going to Aswan on a business trip in a couple of days,' Max said, after a brief pause. 'I suppose I could pick your things up and bring them back with me.'

'Could you?' Bethan brightened up at once. 'I'd be really grateful.'

'That would be a novel experience,' remarked Max caustically. Then he looked down at the food on his plate and gave it a gentle prod. 'What exactly am I eating here?'

'Tinned spam, tinned potatoes and tinned peas. I know it's not very exciting, but it's quite nutritious,' said Bethan defensively. 'And things will get better now Ahmed's been to fetch fresh supplies.'

Max's face clearly told her that he didn't think their meals could get very much worse. Bethan eyed him warily as she tackled her own food. When she had told Max she would take over the cooking, she had thought it would be best not to mention the fact that her experience in culinary matters was very basic, to say the least. Anyway, she was sure she would improve as she gradually got the hand of it.

Peter Wallace raised his head. 'Are you going to Aswan by boat, Max?' he asked, switching the conversation back to an earlier topic.

Max nodded. 'I'll stay overnight in Aswan, then return the next day.'

'Then why not take Bethan with you?' Peter suggested. 'She missed out on her holiday cruise, and a trip up the Nile's a great experience. I'm sure she'd love it.'

Bethan was just about to give a whoop of delight when she saw Max's face. His expression said it all. There was no way he was going to take her with him on that trip. He looked as if he would be quite willing to tie her to a tent post to make absolutely sure she stayed behind!

Glumly, she forked some food into her mouth as she listened to Max smoothly begin to explain why it wasn't at all practical for her to go with him. Peter wasn't swayed by his arguments, though.

'I'm sure we can get round any problems. And perhaps you could take Poppy, as well? She's worked flat out since she's been here. She deserves a couple of days' break.'

Poppy let out an enthusiastic squeal. 'Do you really mean it, Peter?' She turned to Max. 'Do say we can go—it'll be absolutely marvellous!'

A resigned expression began to spread over Max's face. 'I'll be making a very early start,' he warned them discouragingly.

'We'll be up at the crack of dawn,' promised Poppy. 'Won't we, Bethan?'

'The crack of dawn,' agreed Bethan, with a grin.

Max lifted his shoulders in capitulation. 'Then it

looks as if the trip's on.'

From his tone, it was clear he was less than thrilled. He didn't seem totally against it any longer, though. Bethan had the distinct impression that his attitude had changed when Peter had suggested Poppy should join them, to make a threesome. Didn't he want to be alone with her? she wondered with a small, puzzled frown. But why not? There had never been anything between them—well, there had been that one kiss, she reminded herself. But it had meant even less to him than it had to her, she was sure of that. He had probably forgotten all about it by now.

Then she stopped bothering her head about his reasons for not wanting to take her. The trip was going to go ahead, and that was the only important thing. She was going on a cruise up the Nile!

Poppy had a small travelling alarm clock, which they set the night before the trip so they wouldn't over-sleep. When its rather tinny little bell woke Bethan up, it was still dark and quite cold. Shivering slightly, she dragged a blanket round her shoulders; then she hauled herself off the camp bed and went over to Poppy.

'Hey—wake up!'

Poppy's red head emerged from under the blankets, and she gave a small groan. 'I've already been awake for a couple of hours. Can you find me some aspirins?'

'What's the matter?'

'My period's started early, and I feel really rough,' Poppy said glumly. 'Oh, damn, why couldn't it have waited for a couple of days? I was really looking for-ward to that trip up the Nile, and now I feel too rotten to go.'

'I'll stay here with you,' said Bethan sympathet-ically.

'Don't be daft. I'm not dying, I've just got bad

stomach cramp. There's no reason why you should miss the trip, as well.'

'But I can't leave you on your own if you're not feeling well.'

'What are you going to do?' demanded Poppy, with a touch of exasperation. 'Hold my hand and mop my brow? Just find me some aspirins, and then get yourself ready.. Mr Lansdelle hates people being late. If you're not ready on time, he'll go without you.'

Bethan felt rather guilty about leaving Poppy, but Poppy was right. There wasn't much she could do except find her the aspirins. Poppy gulped down a couple, then burrowed back under the blankets, and was fast asleep by the time Bethan tiptoed out of the tent.

She could hear the engine of the Land Rover already ticking over. Realising Max was waiting for her, she hurried over and climbed in beside him.

'Where's Poppy?' asked Max immediately, looking round with a sudden frown.

'She can't come. She's not feeling too good—er —female problems,' Bethan went on tactfully.

Max's frown instantly deepened. Bethan waited apprehensively, wondering if he was going to tell her the trip was cancelled

'You still want to come?' he growled rather tersely at last.

'Of course,' she said immediately.

He gave a brief grunt, which clearly told her he had been hoping for a different answer. To her relief, though, he didn't try to sling her out of the Land Rover. Instead, he put it into gear and drove away from the camp.

As the Land Rover bounced along the deserted, arid valleys, the sun began to inch its way above the low, barren hills, casting long and dramatic shadows. After a while, they reached the main part of the Valley of the Kings. They were on one of the busier tourist routes now, speeding past the tombs of the long-dead pharaohs of Egypt. This early in the morning, there were few people about. Later in the day, though, it would be swarming with people who had come to see the magnificent wall paintings and the remains of the great granite sarcophagi which had once held the mummified bodies of the rulers of this ancient land.

Yet Bethan wasn't thinking about the shadowed splendour of the interiors of those tombs. Instead, a dark frown settled over her face as her thoughts wandered back to Roger, and his revolting groping hands as he had cornered her in one of those underground chambers.

Max glanced at her. 'No happy memories of this place?' he asked perceptively.

'Definitely not!' Bethan grimaced. 'It's a funny business, isn't it? The way we react to other people? I mean, why do some men turn you off straight away, while others have just got to look at you and you feel all sort of queer and melting inside?'

'If anyone could explain that, it would mean they'd solved one of the great mysteries of life,' Max replied drily. 'And it works both ways, of course. Men are often turned on by one particular type of woman. They find it hard to be attracted to anyone who doesn't have the characteristics that spark off that response.'

'What type do you go for?' asked Bethan curiously.

'Blondes,' he answered, after a short pause.

That figured, thought Bethan wryly, remembering Poppy's description of his fiancée. She absently fingered her own glossy black hair. Well, he couldn't have made it any clearer that she definitely wasn't his type! Not that she minded, of course. It was a relief to know that they weren't going to run into any of those sort of problems. It wasn't very flattering to know that she left him cold, but at least it was good for her peace of mind.

They had reached the bank of the Nile by now. Bethan glanced up as Max brought the Land Rover to a halt; then she blinked in astonishment. When he had said they were going by boat, she had pictured something small and functional. She definitely hadn't expected anything like the large, powerful launch moored to the bank.'

'Is that yours?' she asked, still gaping.

'It's only hired,' Max answered absently. 'It comes in useful when we want to cross over to Luxor. It means we don't have to wait for the ferry.'

Bethan began to realise that she had seriously underestimated a lot of things about this man.

'You've hired a boat like this just because it's a bit inconvenient, having to wait for the ferry? she said disbelievingly.

'I don't see that there's anything particularly extraordinary about that.'

'That rather depends on your point of view,' Bethan retorted. 'I mean, would you buy an airline to save you the inconvenience of having to wait for a plane?'

Max lifted one eyebrow. 'I already have my own plane.'

Her own eyebrows shot up. 'I should have guessed! Merchant banking must be a very profitable business.'

'Only if you know what you're doing,' he replied coolly. Then he got out of the Land Rover and went over to the boat.

Bethan trailed after him. As she approached the

boat, a huge man uncurled himself from the deck and stood up, his white robes rather crumpled. He and Max exchanged formal greetings, then Max turned to Bethan.

'This is Rashid. He looks after the boat when we're not using it.'

From the impressive size of him, Bethan guessed that Rashid was very good at frightening off anyone who tried to sneak aboard.

'Is he coming with us to Aswan?' she asked.

Max shook his head. 'He'll return to his village until we come back tomorrow. We don't need him on board. The boat may look large, but it can quite easily be handled by one person.'

Rashid smiled at both of them, then jumped ashore and loped off into the distance. Bethan was rather sorry to see him go. Now there was just her and Max again, and, try as she might, she couldn't quite get rid of a small niggle of unease somewhere deep in the pit of her stomach. There was no need for it; nothing Max had said or done had indicated that she had any cause for alarm—quite the opposite, in fact. Yet it was there, and it refused to go away.

Max was standing on the deck, now. He looked down at her, his dark hair ruffled by the breeze, his strange amber eyes quite unreadable.

'Coming aboard?' he invited.

Bethan hesitated for just a moment longer, and then scrambled up to join him.

CHAPTER FOUR

AS MAX untied the mooring ropes, Bethan peered through the door that led into the main cabin. A moment later, she whistled. Wall-to-wall luxury! After the spartan conditions at the camp, this would be like living at the Ritz.

Max had headed straight for the wheelhouse. He checked over the impressive array of instruments, then he started up the engines, which throbbed softly but powerfully.

'Why don't you take a look around?' he suggested, as he swung the boat away from the bank and headed towards the centre of the river. 'Familiarise yourself with the layout. There's the main cabin, a galley, a couple of small cabins at the front of the boat, and shower and toilet facilities.'

Bethan immediately latched on to the most important word. 'A shower?' she echoed longingly.

He grinned. 'I thought that might interest you. Washing facilities at the camp do tend to be a bit basic. You should find everything you need—soap, towels, shampoo, the lot.'

Several minutes later, Bethan was standing blissfully under the running water. She soaped herself from head to foot, washed her hair, and then sighed with the sheer pleasure of being totally clean again. She could have stood there all day, and only turned off the water with great reluctance.

It was a pity she didn't have anything else to put on

except the borrowed jeans and baggy blouse, but she consoled herself with the thought that she would soon have her own clothes back again. It would be great to wear something that actually fitted!

With a towel wound round her wet hair, she went back up on deck. The sun had fully risen now, and its heat was already driving away the lingering chill of the night. She sat and dried her hair, leisurely pulling a comb through the black strands until they were glossy and dry. Then she just sat and gazed at the scenery: the fields, the palm trees and small villages that fringed the banks, all dependent on the waters of the Nile to nourish them. And beyond the narrow green fringe that supported life was the ever-present desert— ageless, mysterious, and awe-inspiring in its vastness.

Bethan stayed there for ages, drinking it all in. It wasn't until the boat slowed to little more than walking pace that she looked round to see what was happening.

'There's a lock to be negotiated,' Max called out to her. 'How about making some coffee while we're waiting?'

The galley turned out to be well equipped, with a sink, a two-ring gas stove, lots of small, useful gadgets, and even a refrigerator stocked with food. Bethan made the coffee, and there was plenty of time to drink it while they were penned up inside the lock with several other boats, waiting for the water to pour in and carry them up to the upper level. Finally, they were on the move again, slowly making their way past the boats that were waiting on the upstream side of the lock. A couple of them were cruise ships, surrounded by men and boys with thin, dark, handsome faces, and wearing turbans and the traditional *galabeahs*. There was a lot of heated haggling going on as they tried to sell trinkets and souvenirs to the people on the boats. Then Bethan spotted something else, and she gave a sudden yell.

'Max, stop. Stop!'

He immediately cut the engine, then turned his head sharply.

'What is it?'

She pointed towards the quayside. 'Look,' she said excitedly. 'It's a snake-charmer!'

Max's response was brief and extremely rude.

She frowned. 'What's the matter?'

'The way you were yelling, I thought we were sinking, at least. Don't do that again!' he growled irritably. 'I'm not stopping every five minutes so you can look at the bloody sights.'

She was just about to snap back at him when she rather hurriedly stopped herself. He hadn't been too thrilled about her coming on this trip in the first place. She wouldn't put it past him to chuck her off the boat if she annoyed him too much. It was hard to keep her mouth shut—she was used to saying exactly what she thought—but for the next couple of days, it might be prudent to try to curb her impulsive tongue!

The boat was moving faster now, past banks that were thickly studded with palm trees. It was getting too hot to sit out on the deck, but she certainly didn't want to go below and miss any of the scenery, so she made her way to the wheelhouse and plonked herself down in a shady corner. Max didn't even turn his head; he was concentrating on navigating the great river. For a while, Bethan watched him expertly handling the controls of the boat. Then she hurriedly reminded herself that she was meant to be enjoying the splendours of the Nile, not staring at Max, and she dragged her gaze away and concentrated on the fascinating views.

A couple of hours passed in what turned out to be an unexpectedly companionable silence. Then, to her surprise, Max suddenly cut the engines and let the boat drift towards the nearest bank.

'What are we stopping for?' she asked.

'I like to eat occasionally,' pointed out Max. 'And it's well past lunch time.'

'I don't even remember having breakfast,' Bethan replied a little mournfully, realising that she was absolutely starving. 'But are you sure you can spare the time?' she added slightly acidly. 'I thought you didn't intend to stop for anything?'

'I can spare half an hour. Anyway, I haven't got a lot of choice. I can't eat and navigate at the same time.'

'I could take a spell at the wheel,' she offered, 'It can't be very different from driving a car.'

Max merely looked amused. 'You'd soon find out how different it was. And as you pointed out to me earlier this morning, this *is* a very expensive boat.'

'You don't trust me!' Bethan accused indignantly. 'You think I'd steer us straight into the nearest sandbank.'

He shrugged. 'It's possible. Or you might turn out to be an absolute whizz behind the wheel. This isn't a good time to find out, though.' He glanced at his watch. 'It's getting late. Do you want to get the lunch, or shall I?'

Bethan's eyebrows shot up. 'You're offering to do the *cooking?*'

'Is there anything so incredible about that?'

'You just don't look the type,' she told him bluntly.

'What the hell do you mean by that?' His tone was a mixture of amusement and exasperation.

'It's the image you project,' she explained. 'Definitely male macho—you look as if you should be strutting around, telling everyone that a woman's place is in the kitchen. That you don't know how to boil an egg, and what's more, you've got no intention of ever learning.'

Max shook his head in disbelief. 'That's the craziest thing anyone's ever said to me.'

'Perhaps it's just that no one's ever actually had the nerve to say it to your face before,' she said, quite unperturbed.

'And that's one thing you're certainly not lacking in, is it?' he commented drily. 'Nerve?'

'That doesn't exactly sound like a compliment!'

'Perhaps it is—in a rather backhanded way.' Then his voice became businesslike again. 'So, who's to get the lunch? Or do you want to toss for it?'

'It's all right, I'll do it.' She scrambled to her feet, then shot him a sly glance. 'I wouldn't want to ruin your image.'

She whipped up some omelettes, which should have turned out to be light and fluffy, but instead sat soggily on the plate, looking decidedly unappetising. To her relief, though, Max refrained from any comment, and stoically ate his way through the entire plateful. He must have been *very* hungry, Bethan decided, only managing half of hers before giving up. Either that, or he had a cast-iron digestive system.

At least the coffee tasted all right. Although, seeing as it was instant, there wasn't very much she could have done to ruin it.

Max looked at her consideringly as she began to clear away the plates. 'Is there anything you can actually do well?' he asked at last.

Bethan put down the plates. 'What do you mean?'

'Well, you can't cook; you can't climb a cliff without losing your footing and injuring yourself. And from what you've told me, you don't seem much good at coping with men when they corner you in a difficult situation.'

'You just haven't seen me at my best these last few days,' she told him with some dignity.

'So—what are you good at?'

Her dark brows drew together. It was an easy enough question—she should have been able to rattle off an answer. The more she thought about it, though, the more she was forced to conclude that it was the hardest thing she had been asked for a very long while. And the answer that she did finally come up with didn't please her very much.

'I suppose I'm not really good at anything,' she admitted rather grudgingly.

Surprise flickered across Max's face. 'Not many people are willing to admit something like that.'

'What do you want me to do? Lie?'

'You've already done it once!' he reminded her. 'You told me you could cook.'

'I didn't actually say that. I just said that I couldn't be much worse at it than Poppy.'

'I'd say the two of you were roughly on a par,' came his caustic response. Then he looked at her more thoughtfully. 'Why aren't you any good at anything?'

'I suppose it's because everything came easy to me,' she replied frankly. 'It made me lazy. I never bothered to make an effort. I told you I was a spoilt brat, and it's the truth. Practically all my life, I was given everything I wanted. All I had to do was ask. Or make so much fuss, they gave it to me just to keep me quiet,' she added, with a grimace.

'Doting parents?' Max asked.

'Parent, singular,' she corrected him. 'Father, to be

precise. My mother died when I was born. My father wasn't much interested in me—I wasn't the son and heir he'd wanted—but that made him feel guilty, so he tried to make up for it by practically drowning me in material things.'

'And you never refused them?'

'What kid would? I thought it was great. I only had to point at some toy or trinket, and I'd get it.'

'It doesn't sound like the best way to bring up a child,' Max observed. 'Didn't anyone ever tell your father that?'

'They might have done.' Bethan shrugged. 'He wouldn't have bothered to listen. All he was ever interested in was his work. He was hardly ever at home. When he wasn't at the office, he was travelling around on business, going to meetings, setting up new ventures. If I'd been a boy, I suppose it would have been different, he would have taken more interest in me. But since I wasn't . . .'

As her voice trailed away, Max glanced at her sharply. 'Women go into business nowadays,' he reminded her. 'There aren't as many women executives as men, I'll grant you that, but quite a number do make it. If your father wanted an heir, someone who would eventually take over the business he was building up, there was no reason why he shouldn't have taken you on and trained you, shown you how to handle the responsibility and take whatever decisions were needed.'

'He'd never have done that,' Bethan said with absolute certainty. 'He was very old-fashioned in a lot of ways. He thought women should marry, and then spend their lives looking after their husbands and children.'

Max lifted one eyebrow. 'I can't see you as a stay-at-home housewife.'

She grinned. 'Nor can I. Though my father tried
hard enough to marry me off. As soon as I was
eighteen—a marriageable age, in his opinion—an endless stream of eligible young men were paraded in front
of me. Heaven knows where he dredged them all up
from! They turned up everywhere. They arrived for
Sunday lunch, evening meals—even breakfast, sometimes. Some mornings, I was afraid to open the
bathroom door in case I found one lurking in the
shower!'

'Your father must have had your welfare at heart, to
have gone to so much trouble.'

Bethan pulled a face. 'More likely, he just wanted to
get rid of me. I was a bit of a handful by that time,' she
admitted with a wry twist of her mouth. 'I got into all
sorts of trouble, did a lot of very stupid things. He
probably wanted to find me a husband and shunt all
the responsibility on to someone else.'

'Why did you behave so badly?' asked Max, with a
small frown. 'What were you trying to do? Grab your
father's full attention for once in your life?'

She shifted a little restlessly. She couldn't remember
ever talking about herself so frankly before, and it was
beginning to make her feel slightly uncomfortable.

'I suppose that would be a fairly glib explanation,'
she conceded. 'It might even be the true one. If it was,
though, it didn't work. Nothing ever distracted him
from his business interests for very long. After a while,
I just gave up trying. We went our separate ways for a
few months, and each got on with our own lives.' She
paused and swallowed hard. 'Then, one day, I got a
phone call from his office to say he was dead.'

Her blunt statement seemed to have an electrifying
effect on Max. His mouth set into a taut line, and he

visibly stiffened.

'How did he die?' he asked sharply.

'A heart attack. It just came out of the blue, no warning at all. One day he looked perfectly fit and healthy, the next—he was gone.'

Bethan managed to keep her own voice fairly steady. What was the point in getting upset all over again? she told herself fiercely. It was in the past, now; she was over the shock and the unexpected grief. She was even over that awful phase of resentment, when she had been so blindly and unreasonably angry that she was now never going to get a chance to form any sort of loving relationship with the man who had fathered her.

Max was still looking at her with that tense expression. Then he said in a carefully controlled tone, 'Was your father Howard Lawrence?'

Her head shot up in astonishment. 'Yes, he was! How did you know that?'

'It was a guess. When you told me he'd died, I made a connection between the two names.'

'Did you *know* him?'

'Not personally. But I'm a banker,' he reminded her. 'And Howard Lawrence was well known in financial circles.' He hesitated, as if deeply reluctant to say anything more. Finally, though, he went on in a much rougher voice, 'It goes a lot further than that, though. I'm one of the people who was brought in afterwards to help put straight the mess your father left behind when he died.'

Bethan stared at him, her eyes dark with disbelief. '*You?*' She shook her head incredulously. 'I don't believe this!' Then she looked at him with a new defensiveness. 'Then you know all about it? The huge loans, the debts? And I always thought my father was such a marvellous businessman,' she said a little bitterly.

'He was. But he took chances, he gambled. If he hadn't died, he might have pulled off those last deals he made. His name carried a lot of weight. People were willing to trust him, to wait for their money to be repaid. It was all as delicately balanced as a house of cards, though. Once he died, the central card was gone and the whole thing just collapsed.'

She gave a small sigh. 'It's so hard to imagine him taking chances, borrowing such vast sums and gambling that he'd be able to pay them back when the time came. He just wasn't like that in private life. He was always so austere, so unemotional. At least, that's the impression I always got,' she added, with a brief wave of all the old resentment. 'But I saw so little of him, I suppose I didn't know *what* he was really like.'

Max was silent for a couple of minutes. Then he said in a neutral tone, 'This rather changes things, doesn't it? How do you feel about carrying on with this trip? I've got to go on to Aswan—I've a business meeting there this evening—but if you like, I can drop you off at the next town, and you can get a train back to Luxor.'

'Why would I want to do that?' she asked confusedly, still dazed by all these sudden revelations.

'Haven't you been listening to what I've been telling you?' Max's tone was clipped, and his expression was unexpectedly fierce. Then he made an obvious effort to calm himself. 'Your father spent years, working every hour God sent, to build up his string of companies. It probably killed him in the end, because the stresses and strains involved in that sort of intensive hard work are enough to give anyone a heart attack. And in just a few months, I helped to dismantle his entire empire. We stripped everything down to its basic assets, and then sold off as much as we could, to try and cover the worst of the debts. By the time we'd finished, there wasn't anything left. The companies your father had built up went on, but under different names and under new ownership. We saved quite a lot of jobs, but we had to break up a man's dream to do it. And at the end of it, there wasn't anything left for you. We completely stripped you of your inheritance. You were left homeless and penniless. And *I helped to do that.*'

But Bethan just looked at him blankly. She was sure there were all sorts of things she ought to be feeling—shock, outrage, perhaps even astonishment that the two of them should have met like this—but right now, there didn't seem to be anything inside her head except a rather unpleasant numbness.

'Well?' prompted Max, a little harshly. 'Haven't you got anything to say?'

'Did you know about me? I mean, at the time? When you were—you were——'

'When I was selling off what was left of your father's empire? Yes,' he said, with brutal frankness. 'At least, I was aware that Howard Lawrence had a daughter. But I wasn't interested in meeting you, or going to the trouble of finding out anything about you. As far as I was concerned, I was there to do a particular job, and I did it. I realised that you'd be left with absolutely nothing, but if you want the truth, I didn't give it more than a passing thought.'

'You're all heart, aren't you?' Bethan accused.

'I suppose I assumed there would be someone to take care of you, to make sure you didn't actually starve.' His amber eyes fixed on her intently. 'Was there?'

'No,' she said bluntly.

Max lifted his shoulders in a brief shrug. 'What can I say? That I'm sorry? It's rather too late for that.'

'It certainly is!' She stared ahead of her with disturbed eyes. 'You didn't have to tell me all this,' she said finally. 'You could just have kept quiet. I'd probably never have found out.'

'But I didn't keep quiet,' he reminded her. 'And you do know. So, what are you going to do about it?'

'I don't know,' she said slowly. Then she raised her head and looked at him. 'If you had to do it all over again, would you do exactly the same thing?'

'Probably,' Max said evenly.

Her gaze was still fixed on him. 'You're a very cold man,' she said at last. 'Did you know that?'

Then she got up and walked out of the wheelhouse, suddenly wanting to get as far away from him as she possibly could.

She made her way to the very back of the boat. She supposed she ought to be brooding over what he had told her, but instead she just gazed at the sights drifting by, a kaleidoscope of impressions imprinting themselves on her mind. Ancient ruins towering above small villages; they were surrounded by rich, glowing colours—the gold of the sand, the endless blue of the sky, the patches of brilliant green where the waters of the Nile irrigated the parched desert, allowing it to spring to life and cover itself with lush vegetation. And above all, there was the Nile itself, flowing silently and peacefully. The movement of the water had an almost hypnotic effect on her.

After a while, she was surprised to find a strong sense of disappointment sweeping over her. After that rather shaky start, she had begun to feel unexpectedly comfortable with Max Lansdelle. She was ready to admit that there were times when he disconcerted her, even times when he made her feel distinctly on edge. She could cope with that, though, and overall she rather liked having him around. He was stimulating company; she even enjoyed arguing with him. But now there had been this sudden shift in their relationship, and she was being forced to work out just how she felt about it. She resented having to put their relationship under a microscope like this. And it was doubly hard because it was making her look back over a part of her life that she had been trying very hard to put behind her, so she could make a completely fresh start.

It was mid-afternoon before she finally returned to the wheelhouse. Max let his gaze rest on her for just an instant; then he returned his attention to the river.

'Well?' he said a little tersely. 'Have you reached any conclusion?'

'Yes, I have,' Bethan said steadily. She settled herself down in the place she had been sitting in earlier, then she forced herself to look at Max. This was the man who had been instrumental in dismantling her life, her whole future, she reminded herself. Efficiently and dispassionately, he had taken her father's business empire apart. And, on his own admittance, he hadn't given more than a brief passing thought as to how it would affect her, how she would survive on next-to-nothing, when she had been used to so much.

But on the other hand, had life really been so marvellous when she had been swamped with all the material goodies that money could buy? Bethan sighed. No, it certainly hadn't!

'In a funny way, I think you rather did me a favour,' she said at last, to Max. 'Taking everything away from me, and leaving me with nothing.'

His expression darkened. 'You're making it sound as if it was a personal vendetta. It wasn't! I was simply doing my job.'

'I know that. That's what I'm trying to tell you—if you'd just give me a chance!' She took a deep breath, then went on, 'For the first time in my life, I was forced to stand on my own two feet. There was no one there, cash in hand, to bail me out if I got into trouble. I had to make it on my own, and deal with my own mistakes.' She gave a rueful smile. 'To begin with, I didn't like it at all! Everything seemed very grim and gritty, and I'd been used to an easy ride. I'd never even had a steady job before. I'd try something, then just walk out as soon as I got bored or something more interesting turned up. I couldn't do that any more. If I didn't work, then I didn't eat. That was an entirely new experience—and one that took some getting used to!'

'How did you cope with it?'

'I somehow muddled through—there wasn't a lot of choice! Oh, there were days when I moaned and complained,' she admitted frankly, 'but when it came down to it, there wasn't much I could do except just get on with it.'

Max looked at her intently. 'Are things any better for you now?'

'A little. Although life's not exactly thrilling. I live in a one-room flat, and I'm stuck in a job that's well paid, but boring and undemanding.'

'Do you blame me for everything that's happened to you?'

'I'd like to,' she said truthfully. 'But I don't see how I can. Someone had to sort out the mess my father left behind. If it hadn't been you, it would have been someone else. And looking back, I can see the experience has actually been good for me, in a rather brutal sort of way. I'm independent now. And I've certainly learnt the value of money. More than that, though, I think I'm a nicer person. You might not think so,' she said, with the first beginnings of a smile, 'but you didn't know me before. I was an absolute pain!'

'It's refreshing to meet someone who's so ready to admit their own faults,' Max said drily. Then his brows drew together. 'But perhaps it's not too late for me to offer the helping hand I should have given you when your father died. You said you were stuck in a boring job. I can probably help you there. I've got a lot of useful contacts. It wouldn't be hard for me to find you something interesting, a job that would really stretch you and use your talents.'

'No,' Bethan refused at once, very firmly. Then, seeing the quick flash of anger in his eyes because she had turned down his offer so bluntly, she went on, 'Max, I need to make it on my own. I've got this far by myself, and I want to go all the way without any help, so I can say *I've* done it, *I've* finally achieved something in my life.' As Max finally nodded, she breathed a silent sigh of relief. Somehow, it had seemed important to make him understand. 'The trouble is,' she went on, 'I'm totally unqualified. I don't even have any special talents—at least, none that I've found out about yet.'

'Have you got any idea what you'd like to do?'

'None.' She shook her head apologetically. 'I'm a pretty hopeless case, aren't I? What's the phrase the Americans use? "I'm still trying to find myself",' she quoted in a very passable accent. Then she gave a wry grin. 'I'll let you know if I ever manage it!'

'In the meantime, do you want to stay on for the rest of this trip?'

'Yes, I do,' she said, without hesitation. Then her eyes gleamed. 'You weren't expecting me to take this sort of attitude, were you? To be so reasonable?'

'No, I wasn't,' admitted Max.

'What did you think I was going to do? Throw a tantrum? Chuck something at you? Jump overboard?'

His amber gaze glittered in response. 'No. But I was a little worried in case you decided to bite me again!'

Bethan instantly blushed bright red. 'I said that I'd improved,' she muttered. 'I didn't say I was perfect yet!'

'You're not doing too badly.'

The casual compliment made her skin burn an even deeper colour. Confused, she turned her head and gazed at the scenery until the vivid glow had finally faded.

Neither of them said anything more, but the silence that fell between them wasn't uncomfortable. They finally reached Aswan late in the afternoon. Max eased the boat into a mooring alongside several large cruise ships which were already tied up along the waterfront, then they both went ashore.

'Can we go and collect my luggage straight away?' asked Bethan.

Max glanced at his watch, and then frowned. 'There isn't much time before I have to be at my meeting.'

'It won't take long,' she said persuasively. 'And I've *got* to have something else to wear. These clothes Poppy lent me are practically falling off me. You wouldn't want me to walk through the streets of Aswan half-naked, would you?'

'Personally, it wouldn't bother me in the least,' he replied calmly. 'I've already seen you half-naked, remember?' She certainly did, and she felt the heat rushing straight back into her face again. 'It might have a fairly catastrophic effect on the people of Aswan, though,' Max went on. 'In the interest of their peace of mind, perhaps we'd better collect your luggage before we do anything else.'

Bethan gave a grin of satisfaction; then she trotted along beside him as he led the way across the broad corniche road, towards a large hotel at the far end.

It didn't take long for her to be reunited with her missing luggage. She picked up the cases, and then turned to Max.

'Is this where we're staying tonight?'

He shook his head. 'I've already made reservations at another hotel.'

Bethan was rather pleased about that. Although the hotel was spotlessly clean and obviously had all mod cons, it was also very modern and completely lacking in character.

The hotel that Max took them to was the complete opposite. It was of majestic proportions, and had red granite walls that positively glowed in the light of the setting sun. It was set in the middle of beautiful gardens that stretched right down to the river, and there was a long, shady terrace that looked marvellously inviting after the intense heat that had beaten down on them all day.

'This is more like it,' she murmured appreciatively.

Max heard her, and grinned. 'It's an interesting place to stay. And it won't be crammed full of tourists.'

Bethan's brows immediately drew together in a quick frown. 'Because it's too expensive?' she guessed at once. 'Then I won't be able to afford it, either. I'd better find somewhere else.'

She turned round, ready to leave, but Max caught hold of her arm.

'I'm paying,' he told her.

'No, you're not!' came her instant response.

He gave her a slightly exasperated shake. 'Independence is all very well, but there's no need to carry it to extremes. If Poppy had been able to come, I'd have paid for her, as well. Don't start being irritatingly stubborn over this.'

'I just don't like it!'

'You don't have to like it. All you've got to do is to walk inside and get booked in. And get a move on. If we waste much more time, I'm not going to make my meeting.' His eyes gleamed brightly for a moment. 'Of course, if you're really worried about the cost, we could always share a room,' he suggested smoothly. 'That would certainly work out very much cheaper.'

'Now you're making fun of me,' she accused, with a scowl.

A strange expression crossed Max's face. Then it vanished again without a trace. 'Of course I am,' he agreed. 'We'll have separate rooms—even different floors, if you like. Just shift yourself, Bethan!'

Inside, the hotel fully lived up to its impressive façade. High ceilings, stone floors, huge fans instead of the usual air-conditioning, and a delightful ambience of faded elegance. After they had signed in, Max turned to her.

'I'm going up to shower and change, then I'm going straight to my meeting. I probably won't be back until late, since I'll almost certainly be invited to my client's house for an evening meal. Hospitality's a big part of any business negotiations in this part of the world. It would be considered extremely discourteous if I refused, and it could well put the whole deal in jeopardy. The hotel has its own restaurant, so you can have your own meal there. Just ask them to put it on my bill.'

'Couldn't I come with you?' Bethan suggested hopefully 'I'd love to see inside an Egyptian home and try some genuine local food.'

Max shook his head. 'It's not possible.'

'Why not? I wouldn't embarrass you or let you down. I've got very good table manners. And I promise not to pull a face or turn green if they give me something really exotic—or disgusting!—to eat.'

'It's not that. This is an Islamic country,' he reminded her, 'and they've got very strict rules regarding women—particularly if they're unmarried. It would be considered most improper—even insulting— if I turned up tonight with an unchaperoned woman on my arm.'

She wrinkled her nose. He was right, of course.

'OK, I give in,' she said, with some disappointment. 'I'll have dinner here, at the hotel.' She picked up her room key. 'See you in the morning.'

She went up to her room, had a long shower, and then opened her suitcase. With a sigh of pleasure, she took out her clothes. They were a little crumpled after their long journey, but still a great improvement on Poppy's baggy jeans and blouses.

She had only one dress that would be suitable for dinner in a hotel like this. It was a little white number, so simple in design that it never looked out of date, even though she had bought it long before her father died. She slipped it on, then went confidently downstairs, knowing that she looked good. The soft white material showed off her dark hair and eyes, her lightly tanned skin, to perfection.

Because she was still rather disappointed that she hadn't been able to go with Max, she cheered herself up by ordering the most expensive dishes from the menu. The meal was excellent, but it would have been much more interesting if she could have spent the evening with an Egyptian family.

The meal was served at such a leisurely pace that it was quite late by the time she finally returned to her room. It had been a long day—and a slightly fraught one!—but, surprisingly, she wasn't tired. What she really wanted to do was to go out and explore, but she had enough sense to know that it wouldn't be at all wise to go wandering through the streets of a strange city at this time of night.

She dug a paperback out of her suitcase and read until her eyes finally began to feel heavy. Giving a tiny yawn, she got to her feet and was just about to get ready for bed when there was a light knock on her door. Bethan's brows drew together in a quick frown. It was rather late at night for visitors—at least, any that would be welcome! She went over to the door and cautiously opened it; then she let out a sigh of relief when she saw it was only Max on the other side.

'You scared me half to death! I thought it was some wealthy Egyptian, come to proposition me.' She gave him a quick grin. 'I wasn't going to surrender my virtue in return for anything less than a large herd of camels.' Then she let her gaze run over him. It was the first time she had seen him dressed so formally, in a dark suit and white silk shirt, and with gold cuff-links glinting at his wrists. 'Very impressive! In a suit like that, you couldn't help but clinch your deal.'

'Nothing's been signed yet, but all the negotiations are running smoothly,' Max agreed.

'I'm pleased to hear it, but did you come knocking on my door at gone midnight just to tell me what a brilliant businessman you are?'

'Is it that late?' asked Max, looking a little surprised. 'I didn't realise——' He glanced at his watch.

'I'd better let you get to bed. I just wanted to tell you that there's no need for you to get up at the crack of dawn in the morning. We can leave around nine and still be back at the camp by evening.'

'I'll see you at breakfast, then.'

'No, you won't.' A glint of mischief lit up his amber eyes. 'I've arranged for you to have breakfast in bed. A special treat,' he added generously.

Bethan regarded him suspiciously. Somehow, she didn't trust him when he was being so considerate. Then she decided she was being uncharitable. He was probably just trying to make up for leaving her on her own all evening.

'Thank you,' she said politely. 'Goodnight.'

He didn't leave immediately, though. Instead, he leant forward, and let the lightest of kisses brush against the smooth skin of her forehead.

'Goodnight, Bethan.' Then he finally turned and walked away.

Bethan slowly closed the door. That was the second time he had kissed her.

Then she shook her head rather impatiently. It hadn't meant anything. The first time, he had kissed her just to teach her a lesson. And that brief touch of his lips a few moments ago had been the sort of kiss he might have given to a young child; a casually affectionate gesture that had absolutely no significance.

Yet, as she got ready for bed, she couldn't help wondering what his third kiss would be like—if it ever came.

CHAPTER FIVE

NEXT morning, she was awakened by a discreet tap on her door. Yawning hard, she sat up and rubbed her eyes; then she remembered Max's promise of breakfast in bed. It must be one of the hotel staff with her breakfast tray.

Realising she was starving, she quickly pulled on a light robe and then called to the girl outside to come in.

As the door opened, Bethan glanced up; then she let out a high squeak of alarm which she hurriedly tried to turn into a cough. It *was* her breakfast tray—but it most certainly wasn't a girl who was carrying it. Instead, it was a huge Nubian! He was seven foot if he was an inch, with skin like polished ebony, very handsome features, and a dignified expression. His bare feet moved silently over the tiled floor, his spotless robe swung softly with every graceful movement, and the tassel on his fez drooped forward as he leant over to put the tray down on the table. Then he gave a small, polite bow, and glided out of the room again.

For several moments after he had gone, shutting the door noiselessly behind him, Bethan just stood there with her eyes as huge as saucers. Then she dissolved into helpless laughter. She had seen several of the giant Nubians around the hotel yesterday evening, quietly and efficiently attending to the needs of the guests. She just hadn't realised that one of them would also be bringing her breakfast in bed!

She ate hungrily, showered and changed, and then

finally made her way downstairs. Max was already there, waiting for her.

'Did you enjoy your breakfast?' he asked, with a perfectly straight face.

'It was—very interesting,' she answered, her eyes dancing.

'I thought you might appreciate it. It's one of the more interesting features of this hotel.' Then his tone became more brisk. 'Come on, we'd better make a start or we won't be back at the camp before it gets dark.'

Bethan was rather reluctant to leave Aswan without seeing the cataracts, the High Dam, or getting a chance to explore the *souks* and browse through the leather goods and pretty jewellery, the brass ornaments, the spices and brightly coloured cotton goods. Max obviously intended to leave straight away, though. If she wanted to return to the camp, she didn't have much choice except to go with him.

Once back on the boat, though, with the powerful engines throbbing and the banks of the Nile slipping past like vivid scenes from an exotic travelogue, she soon settled down. They stopped just once, for a quick lunch, but less than half an hour later they were off again.

It was about half-way through the afternoon when Bethan noticed that the weather seemed to be changing. The sky wasn't the clear, radiant blue it had been all morning—and every morning since her arrival in Egypt. Instead, it was turning a rather odd sort of grey, with yellowish tinges. Even the waters of the Nile seemed to be changing colour, taking on a distinctly greenish hue which, for the first time, made the river appear just a little ominous.

Bethan made her way to the wheelhouse, and found

that Max had also noticed the changes. He was frowning irritably as he studied the sky, and he had eased off on the throttle, so the boat was moving noticeably slower.

'Is it going to rain?' she asked curiously.

'No,' he said shortly. 'It's the *khamsin* wind.'

'Oh, well, if it's just a bit of a breeze——' she said in a relieved tone.

'The *khamsin* can blow for several days on end,' Max informed her concisely. 'And it often whips up dust and sandstorms.'

Bethan swallowed hard. 'Several days?'

Max was no longer paying any attention to her. Instead he headed the boat towards the nearest bank, and then cut the engines.

'We'll have to anchor here until it's passed. And let's hope the damn thing doesn't last too long,' he growled.

Bethan stood around, feeling totally useless while he anchored the boat and then made it as secure as he could. The wind was picking up all the time now and, after a while, they went below. When all the doors and portholes were tightly shut, Max switched on the air-conditioning so that it wouldn't get unbearably hot and stuffy.

'I'll make some coffee,' Bethan offered helpfully. 'It looks as if we're going to be stuck here for quite a while.'

It was while they were drinking the coffee that the sandstorm hit them. The tiny particles of sand and grit swept endlessly against the boat, setting up an eerie hissing that went on and on until Bethan's nerves began to feel positively frayed. On top of that, the boat was rocking continuously now as it was buffeted by the strong gusts of wind. She was just grateful that she was turning out to have a strong stomach. It would have been the last straw if she had been seasick!

Max was hardly the ideal companion at the moment, either. He had scarcely said a word since the sandstorm had struck, and right now he was just sitting there, gazing broodingly ahead of him, as if she wasn't even there.

Bethan tried to think of some topic of conversation that would interest him, and jolt him out of his introspective mood.

'Tell me something about merchant banking,' she said at last, in a determined effort to break the silence.

He shot her a rather disbelieving look. 'Are you really interested?'

'Yes, I am,' she insisted firmly. 'Isn't it—well, a little dull?' Try as she might, she couldn't picture this restless, vital man sitting behind a desk all day, shuffling pieces of paper.

Max's amber eyes lit with sudden amusement as his sombre mood lifted.

'Dull? No, I don't think you could call it dull. Not unless you think it's boring to gamble with vast sums of money.'

She instantly looked rather shocked. 'How can you say banking is like gambling?'

'It's not a description that many bankers would approve of,' he conceded. 'But it's how I've always seen it.'

'But you only lend money, don't you?' Bethan said doubtfully. 'Where's the risk in that?'

'There's always the chance that we won't be repaid,' Max responded drily. 'And we don't run individual accounts, like the commercial banks, where the sums involved are usually fairly small. Basically, we lend money to businesses who come to us wanting to raise capital, perhaps to expand or to fund some new project. No matter how sound those schemes might sound on paper, there's nearly always an element of risk involved; some factor, either predictable or unpredictable, which can make them go disastrously wrong. What I have to do is to calculate just how much risk is involved, and then decide whether the bank should go ahead with the financing. If I get it wrong, then we lose a great deal of our money—perhaps all of it.'

'Have you ever made a really major mistake?'

'No. Only a couple of minor ones. And they were quite a long time ago.'

She might have guessed that, she thought to herself, pulling a wry face. Max Lansdelle wasn't the type of man to make serious mistakes!

The conversation began to lag again after that, and the rest of the afternoon dragged by, with no sign of a let-up in either the wind or the sandstorm it was whipping up. The prospect of having to stay here all night was beginning to loom ahead of them, and she had the distinct feeling that Max found that idea as unappealing as she did.

As evening drew in, she occupied herself for a while by making them a meal. At least they wouldn't starve, she consoled herself. There was enough food here to last them a month. Once they had eaten, though, there was little to do except sit and listen to the sand hissing against the outside of the boat. Max didn't seem to want to talk—in fact, he seemed oddly restless, prowling up and down, then scowling fiercely out of the porthole at the storm, until he thoroughly got on her nerves. Why couldn't he just sit still for five minutes? He was making *her* feel on edge, pacing up and down like some caged animal.

In the end, she got completely fed up with it. 'I'm going to bed,' she announced. 'Shall I use the small cabin?'

'If you like,' came his curt reply.

'Look, there's no need to act as if this whole thing's my fault,' she retorted irritably. 'I don't like being stuck here any more than you do.'

He looked as if he was about to say something. Then he turned away from her with a brief, impatient gesture of his hands. 'Bethan, just go to bed!'

She was about to make a sharp reply when she gave a small shrug and stopped herself. It was no use trying to argue with a man who had rather pointedly turned his back on you. Anyway, she didn't even know what they were arguing about. She supposed they had just started to get on each other's nerves, cooped up together in this confined space. When she had first seen the boat yesterday, she had thought it was large and quite spacious. These last few hours, though, it had somehow seemed to be shrinking, closing in on them, until they couldn't seem to move without getting under each other's feet. No wonder they were snapping at one another and getting edgy. The best thing she could do would be to take herself off to her cabin. That would give her and Max a few hours apart, and a chance to get back their equilibrium.

Even with the air-conditioning going, it seemed warm and stuffy inside the small cabin. Bethan thankfully stripped off her clothes and wriggled into a cool cotton nightie. Then she stretched out on the narrow bunk bed and tried to read. She couldn't concentrate, though. After a while, she chucked the book to one side and peered out of the porthole.

She couldn't see a thing. Darkness had wrapped itself round the boat like a huge black blanket. Nor could she hear anything except that nerve-grating hissing as millions of grains of sand were hurled against the glass. Wishing she had some cotton wool to shove in her ears to block out the infuriating sound, she buried her head in the pillow and tried to sleep.

For ages, she lay there with her eyes tightly shut, trying to convince herself that she was tired and would fall asleep at any moment. At last, though, she had to admit that it wasn't going to work. She was still absolutely wide awake. What was more, she was getting thirsty.

She swung herself off the bunk bed. There were cartons of fresh orange juice in the galley. Perhaps she would be able to sleep after she had had a drink.

She padded, barefooted, along to the galley, and was about to go inside when she noticed a thin ribbon of light showing under the door that led to the main saloon. After a moment's hesitation, she walked over and opened it.

Max was stretched out on the long, low seat which ran right along the far side. As she came in, he glanced up, and she saw that his amber eyes seemed far brighter than she ever remembered seeing them.

'I was just going to get myself a drink,' she explained. 'Do you want one?' Then her gaze slid down to the bottle and empty glass that stood on the table in front of him. 'Oh,' she said slowly, understanding now why his gaze seemed so brittle and brilliant. 'I see you've already had one. Or two. Or was it three?'

'I haven't been counting,' Max drawled. 'But there's no need to throw that censorial look at me. I'm not drunk. And even if I were, you wouldn't have any cause for alarm. I never lose control.'

'Do I look alarmed?' she demanded.

Amusement flickered briefly across his face. 'No, you don't,' he agreed. 'Whatever other emotions I might arouse in you, fear certainly isn't one of them.'

'You don't arouse any emotions in me at all,' Bethan told him sharply, suddenly on edge for no reason she could put her finger on. 'Except perhaps exasperation,' she added. 'There are times when you make me totally mad.'

'I wish I could say the same thing,' he murmured.

Bethan looked at him warily. 'What do you mean by that?'

He gave a brief and rather impatient shake of his head. 'Nothing. You're right, I've had too much to drink.'

'Why don't you go to bed and sleep it off?'

His mouth curled into a thin smile. 'I don't feel like sleeping.'

'Then what *do* you feel like?'

Max looked at her with eyes that were suddenly far too revealing. 'Bethan, I think that's one question that you shouldn't ask,' he told her succinctly. 'And that I definitely shouldn't answer.'

She felt a small wave of shock run through her. He couldn't mean——No, of course he didn't, she told herself firmly. He was just teasing her again. Anyway, he had other commitments. And maybe this was a good time to remind him of that.

'It might not be a good idea to tell your fiancée about this little jaunt,' she said, careful to keep her tone light and casual. 'She might take it the wrong way if she hears we've been cooped up together on this boat. Not that she'd have anything to worry about,' she added meaningfully. 'So far, you've behaved like a perfect gentleman.'

Max instantly looked displeased. 'Who told you

about Caroline?' he growled.

'It's not a secret, is it? And even if it is, I'm afraid you've blown it. Apparently, she's a friend of Steve's older sister.'

'No, it isn't a secret,' Max said at last. 'It's just that nothing's official yet.'

'When are you going to make it official?'

'That's none of your damn business!'

'No, I suppose it isn't,' she agreed cheerfully. 'Are you planning to have a big wedding?'

'Bethan!'

'Sorry,' she said, although her voice certainly didn't sound apologetic. 'I really am interested, though. Do your parents approve of your choice?'

Max had begun to look both exasperated and resigned, as if he knew perfectly well that there was no chance of escaping this grilling, much as he disliked it.

'My parents approve of most things I do nowadays.'

'Wasn't that always the case?' she asked with some curiosity.

'No, it wasn't.' For a couple of minutes, she didn't think he was going to say anything more. Then he gave a small shrug, and went on, 'When I was younger, I didn't have the slightest interest in banking. And that didn't go down too well, since the name of Lansdelle had been associated with banking for the last four generations. On top of that, I was an only child —the heir apparent,' he added, with a touch of self-mockery. 'From the day I was born, it was taken for granted that I'd follow in the family tradition.'

'But that wasn't what you wanted?' asked Bethan, in some surprise.

'During my teens, I thought it was the very last thing I wanted. I fought against it like hell, deliberately failed exams, did everything I could to convince people that there was no way they were ever going to get me into banking.'

'What did your parents do?'

His mouth curled into a rueful smile. 'What all wise parents do with rebellious children. They gave me my head, and just hoped I'd eventually burn it right out of my system. And that's exactly what happened, of course. The risks, the intricacies and complex negotiations involved in banking all very gradually began to fascinate me. The more I became involved in it, the more I was hooked. Now I'm a Lansdelle through and through—a banker to my fingertips.'

Bethan looked at him shrewdly. 'And now, I suppose you're expected to produce an heir? To carry on the family tradition?'

'A lot of heavy hints have been dropped in that direction,' he agreed. 'Not that I'd force any child of mine into a career. I'd want them to choose for themselves. I'll admit, though, that I'd be very pleased if one—or more—of them became interested in the world of finance.'

Her eyebrows shot up at that. 'Exactly how many children are you planning on having?'

Max's gaze grew very cool. 'I don't think that concerns anyone except myself and my future wife.'

'No, I suppose not,' Bethan agreed, accepting the reprimand in good grace. Then she lifted her head again and studied him thoughtfully. 'You're really a very conventional man, aren't you?'

'Just occasionally, I surprise people by doing what's expected of me.'

'Like getting engaged to a beautiful blonde?' She wondered why her voice suddenly sounded a little strained. 'I bet she's got a pedigree stretching back for ever, loads of class, and absolutely perfect manners.

The ideal wife for a banker,' Bethan said, with a small sniff. Then she couldn't help adding, 'What made you propose to her?'

Rather to her surprise, he answered her. 'I felt it was the right time in my life to get married,' he said slowly. 'I find I'm getting tired of brief relationships, no matter how pleasant they may be at the time. I want a settled home, a family.'

Bethan tilted her head slightly to one side. 'That all sounds very calculated. You haven't once mentioned love.'

'You told me once I was a cold man,' he reminded her. 'And you could well be right. I've seen too many marriages fail because they're based on nothing else except a brief flash of passion. It's far better to choose someone who understands your lifestyle, who comes from the same sort of background and shares mutual friends.'

She shook her head doubtfully. 'That doesn't seem a very good way to choose a marriage partner —at least, not to me. And I'm not sure I was right about you being cold. Sometimes, you pretend to be. Then something in your eyes gives you away.'

Max's expression suddenly changed. Rather abruptly, he got to his feet. 'How the hell did we get involved in this ridiculous conversation?' he said with unexpected curtness. Then he gave a brief scowl. 'It's probably because I'm not as sober as I like to think I am.'

'Then why not go the whole way and get totally legless?' she suggested cheerfully. 'You're nearly always so—oh, so controlled. I'm sure it can't be good for you. Even bankers ought to let off steam once in a while.'

Max shifted his position, so he was standing much

closer than he had been before, and his eyes suddenly glittered. 'You might not like it if I did ever lose control,' he warned softly.

'Well, I wasn't planning on staying around to watch you drink yourself under the table,' she said, a slightly edgy note creeping into her voice.

'But what if I wanted you to stay?'

Was he throwing down a challenge? Well, it was one that she certainly didn't intend to pick up!

'You like blondes,' she reminded him. 'Look at me. Black hair, dark eyes—I'm definitely not your type, Max. You don't want me around.'

'Wrong, Bethan,' he contradicted her. 'Right now, you look *exactly* my type.'

'That's because you've had too much to drink. Besides, I don't——'

'Don't what?' he prompted silkily. 'Don't want to stay?' He took a step closer. 'But how do you know, if you don't give it a try?'

Bethan felt her pulses begin to thump away at top speed. She hadn't expected this; she hadn't been prepared for it.

Just turn away from him and walk out the door, she told herself shakily. That's all you've got to do. He won't come charging after you. He isn't *that* interested; he's just had a bit too much to drink, and it's making him feel amorous.

Yet, somehow, that seemed too glib an explanation for what was happening between them. Max took yet another step towards her, and this brought him within touching distance. His face was only inches away, now. As she stared up into his dark features, she had the strangest feeling that she was seeing him for the first time.

She tried to convince herself that was nonsense.

She was already perfectly familiar with that brooding face with its distinctive brows, intense gaze, straight nose and the curved line of mouth. And those eyes— hungry eyes, she had called them once. It was there again tonight, that hot light she had caught brief glimpses of before, when he was off guard.

'We shouldn't——' she began in an unsteady voice.

'No, we shouldn't,' he agreed. His tone was husky, and she began to panic. Just how much *had* he had to drink?

Then there wasn't any more time to worry about it because, with a brief, impatient movement, he bent his head and inflicted a kiss on her that was rough and yet totally pleasurable, demanding and yet stopping well short of being brutal.

The third kiss, Bethan told herself dazedly. She had wondered about it—and now it was happening. Then all rational thought was swept away as something inside Max suddenly seemed to switch gear. His breathing altered, his body tensed, and his kiss abruptly turned into something very different.

She found herself crushed against him, breasts aching as they were flattened against the hardness of his chest. His fiercely exploring mouth cut off any muffled protests; his tongue insinuated itself between her lips and licked away any remnants of resistance. For what seemed like an incredibly long time, she couldn't do anything except melt against him, the warm contact of her body igniting a hot response which both frightened her with its insistent pressure and yet filled her with an odd sense of exhilaration.

Then his hands began to move much more purposefully, making her gasp out loud. The sound of her own voice briefly brought her back to reality. The waves of pleasure receded for just a few moments; their beguiling influence loosened their grip on her, and her head cleared just enough for her to realise what was happening.

'No,' she said, in an uncertain voice. Then, much more firmly, 'No!'

Max immediately released her.

'Why?'

That single word made her stare at him fiercely. 'I don't have to give you any reasons! I'm just telling you that I don't want this to go any further.'

He lifted his hand, and let his fingertips drift lightly over her hard nipple. 'That's not the message I'm getting.'

With an enormous effort, she stopped herself from shivering in response to that brief but lethal touch; then she stepped back from him.

'I don't care what messages you're getting. I'm telling you how things are going to be.'

The amber eyes suddenly hardened, and he became very still.

'Then perhaps you'd better get back to your cabin. Right now!'

Bethan didn't need telling twice. For her own peace of mind, she needed to get out of here as quickly as she could.

'And there's a lock on the door,' Max growled after her. 'If you've got any sense, you'll use it.'

It was a piece of advice that she had no hesitation in accepting. After she had fled back to her cabin, she turned the key and then just stood there, still breathing unevenly.

The third kiss, she thought again, in total confusion. She had had no idea it would be like that. She couldn't possibly have known what it would do to her.

Slowly, she climbed into bed; then she lay there,

quietly shaking. Did he know just how much effort it had taken to say the word 'No' tonight? And, even more frightening than that, did he know how close she had come to not saying it at all?

Ages later, she finally dozed for a while. When she woke up again, she found the wind had dropped, the sandstorm had blown itself out, and bright sunshine was streaming in through the porthole. The clear, bright light seemed to help her get everything back into perspective again. Sitting up, she congratulated herself on having behaved sensibly last night, and conveniently forgot that it had been touch and go for a while.

It had been the wind and the sandstorm that had triggered the situation in the first place, she told herself firmly. Conditions like that always made people act out of character; it was a well-known phenomenon. Max was no doubt feeling as relieved as she was that they hadn't let the whole thing get out of hand. That was if he was in a condition to think about anything at all this morning, she told herself wryly. He probably had a monumental hangover and couldn't think of anything except his aching head!

She quickly washed and dressed, but then she found she was rather reluctant to go up on deck. Don't be stupid, she lectured herself impatiently. Max isn't some ogre. When you're not fighting with him—and when he's sober—you really get along with him quite well.

She could hear the steady throb of the engines, so she knew Max was up and that they were already under way. Taking a deep breath, she left the cabin and made her way to the wheelhouse.

If Max had a hangover this morning, he was

certainly showing no outward sign of it. As he glanced over at her, she saw his eyes were perfectly clear. And, to her relief, they were looking at her coolly and calmly. There was no trace of that inner blaze which sometimes lit them, and which always made her feel so uneasy when she saw it.

'How long before we get back?' she asked.

'A couple of hours. We've been under way for quite a while.' He hesitated briefly, then added, 'You overslept.'

'I had trouble getting to sleep,' she said, without thinking. Then she felt the colour burn its way into her face. 'It was the sandstorm,' she lied, a little defiantly. 'It kept me awake.'

From the expression on his dark features, it was obvious he didn't swallow that story. 'Do you want me to apologise for last night?' he said without preamble.

She tried to keep her tone very casual. 'For what? You'd had too much to drink, that's all. It happens sometimes.'

'But not usually to me.'

No, I bet it doesn't! she thought to herself silently. Max Lansdelle was the type of man who liked to know exactly what he was doing. He would be angry with himself for the way he had behaved last night. And perhaps angry with her, partly blaming her for what happened.

A little tensely, she waited to see what he would say next. He remained silent, though, and she quickly got the message. This particular conversation was over. From now on, he intended to behave as if nothing of any importance had happened. And he obviously expected her to do the same.

Well, that wouldn't be too difficult, she told herself stiffly. Nothing important *had* happened. Max had kissed her, that was all. She had been kissed before, and would no doubt be kissed again. It was no big thing. Max was pretty good at it—she had to admit that, reluctantly—but since he had obviously had a great deal of practice, she shouldn't find that very surprising.

All the same, she decided to steer clear of Max for the rest of the journey. She found a shady patch at the back of the boat, and then settled down to enjoy the rest of the trip. Somehow, though, the scenery didn't hold her attention the way it had before. All too often, she found her thoughts wandering off in a distinctly disturbing direction.

She was rather glad when they finally arrived back at camp. Clambering out of the Land Rover, she made her way directly to the tent she shared with Poppy, where she slumped down tiredly on her bed.

Poppy came in a couple of minutes later. 'Have a good trip?' she asked enviously. 'I bet it was quite an experience.'

Bethan raised one eyebrow. 'It certainly was,' she agreed, with some feeling. Then, not wanting Poppy to get the wrong impression, she added hurriedly, 'We got caught in a sandstorm. Luckily, it only lasted for a few hours. If it had gone on for days, I'd probably have ended up climbing the walls.'

'I don't think I'd have minded too much if I'd been stuck on a boat with Max Lansdelle,' Poppy said, with a grin. 'All sorts of things could happen in that kind of situation!'

To her annoyance, Bethan could feel the colour seeping into her face. It was a good thing it was getting dark, making the interior of the tent too dim for Poppy to see that infuriating blush.

'I was just glad when it was over,' she insisted firmly.

Then, determined to change the subject—and quickly—she added, 'By the way, how do you feel now?'

'Fine. It's usually only the first day that I feel like death.' Poppy pulled a face. 'I'm really sick about missing that trip.' She flopped down on her own bed, then gave an enormous yawn. 'I think I'll turn in early. We've all put in a hard day's work, and I'm completely flaked out.'

'Have you found anything interesting yet?'

'Not so far. We've drawn a total blank in this new area we've been excavating. I don't know what Peter was hoping to find, but he's looking pretty depressed.'

As Poppy closed her eyes and drifted off almost immediately into a deep sleep, Bethan stared through the open tent flaps at the shadow-filled valley outside. So, Peter hadn't found any trace of the lost tomb for which he was looking. She wondered how long he would go on searching before he finally gave up. A few minutes later, she gave a small sigh and stretched out on her own camp bed. She closed her eyes and, like Poppy, fell asleep straight away.

In the morning, she slept late. By the time she finally stumbled out, bleary-eyed and hungry, Peter Wallace was the only one still around in camp. He was sitting with his uneaten breakfast in front of him, and looking distinctly gloomy.

'Aren't you going to eat that?' asked Bethan, seating herself opposite him.

'I'm not hungry.'

'Mind if I have it?'

He pushed the plate towards her. 'Go ahead.'

She tucked in ravenously for a while, then finally glanced up at him sympathetically. 'You haven't found anything yet?'

'Not a thing.' He looked at her with unexpected sympathy. 'You're probably finding the whole thing extremely boring. Are you sure you want to stick around?'

She stared at him guardedly. 'What do you mean?'

Peter shrugged. 'Just that you probably thought it was going to be a lot more exciting than this. I'd quite understand if you wanted to leave.'

And who had planted that idea in Peter's head? Bethan asked herself furiously. The answer wasn't too difficult to work out! Who was the one person who would find life a lot more uncomplicated if she wasn't around?

'I've no intention of leaving,' she told him firmly. 'You're right, it's not as exciting as I thought it was going to be, but I'm still going to stay.'

And let him deliver that message straight back to Max Lansdelle! she thought to herself angrily. Better still, she would tell him herself.

Max was away from the camp for most of the morning, though. It was gone noon before she saw his Land Rover finally returning. As soon as he got out, she marched over and planted herself in front of him.

'Has Peter delivered my message yet?' she demanded.

Max's own gaze remained very cool. 'What message?'

'That I intend to stay.' Her tone became scornful. 'That was pretty devious, getting him to do your dirty work.'

Max's mouth began to set itself into an impatient line. 'Bethan, it's too hot to stand around trying to work out riddles. Just tell me what the hell you're on about.'

'You don't want me around, so you tried to find a

way of levering me out of here,' she accused. 'That
was very clever, getting Peter to try and convince me it
was so boring around here that I might as well leave.
Unfortunately—for you!—it didn't work. I'm not
going.'

A dark glower spread over Max's features as he
finally understood what she was on about.

'I don't need Peter—or anyone else—to act as my
messenger boy!' he growled. 'If I've got something to
say to you, then I'll say it to your face.'

'I'm right, though, aren't I?' she persisted. 'You
don't want me around.'

'No, I don't. But I'm not going to try and force you
out of here, not if you really don't want to go.'

His answer threw her off balance. She hadn't been
expecting him to say anything like that. 'You're not?'
A note of uncertainty suddenly crept into her voice.
'But—why?'

Max's gazed fixed on her fiercely. 'Because I inter-
fered in your life before, and I'm not going to do it
again.' He held up one hand as she opened her mouth
to argue with him, and she rather hurriedly shut up.
'When I sorted out your father's financial affairs, I
turned *your* life upside-down at the same time. Rather
late in the day, I'm starting to feel guilty about that. I
should have made an effort to find out more about
you, to make sure you were all right. Admittedly, there
wouldn't have been much I could have done—there
wasn't anything I could have salvaged for you from the
financial mess—but by ignoring your existence completely, I didn't discharge my duty properly.'

She stared at him in disbelief. 'Let's get this
straight. You're starting to feel *responsible* for me? But
it's nearly two years since my father died!'

'And on your own admittance, you haven't been

making out too well in that time.'

'I've been doing all right,' she insisted stubbornly.

'You're in a dead-end job, and the last couple of years have been pretty rough,' Max pointed out concisely.

'And you think that's your fault?'

'Partly—yes. If I'd been more helpful at the time of your father's death, you might be in a much better position right now. I could have given you useful advice, helped you find a decent job——'

'And what if I hadn't wanted to accept any help from you?'

Max briefly shrugged his shoulders. 'That would have been your prerogative. But at least I would have tried.'

'And now you've got a guilty conscience about the way you behaved?' Bethan said disbelievingly.

'Let's just say that I don't want to make things worse for you. You're right, I don't like having you around—and I think you know why,' he added, that dark glow flaring in his eyes again. 'But if you're determined to stay, then I'll go along with it. It's your life, Bethan, and you've earned the right to do what you want with it. I shan't interfere a second time.'

With that, he turned and strode off. Bethan just stared after him in amazement. Max Lansdelle being reasonable? Now, that really was something to make everyone keel over with shock!

Had he really meant what he had said? she wondered suspiciously. He had certainly sounded very convincing. It was just so hard to swallow, though. And was there any guarantee that he wouldn't change his mind again tomorrow? There was an unpredictable streak in Max that always seemed to surface just when she was least expecting it.

She finally decided she would go along with it—for now. But she still didn't entirely trust him. Nor was she convinced that he didn't have some ulterior motive in allowing her to stay.

CHAPTER SIX

DESPITE all Bethan's misgivings, the next couple of days passed without too many problems. Since she had a lot of free time, she began to read some of Poppy's books. They were all about archaeology and great archaeological discoveries, and most of them were heavy going. Then she found a couple that were written in a much livelier style, with plenty of colour photographs to accompany the text, and these were much more interesting. Bethan lapped up the stories of old tombs being discovered and their treasures revealed; ancient curses which were either scoffed at or fervently believed; the predictions that there were still many marvels hidden under the shifting sands, just waiting to be dug up.

The following evening, she sat and read until quite late in the evening. She wasn't particularly tired, and there wasn't anything else to do except get on with her book. On the other side of the tent, Poppy was flopped out on her own bed, fast asleep after several long hours of toiling away under the hot Egyptian sun. Even the light from the lamp, by which Bethan was reading, hadn't been enough to keep her awake.

Bethan turned over the page and glanced at one of the photographs. Then she suddenly stared at it again more intently. Something about it had sent a spark of memory flashing through her brain. She turned to the text under the photo, read it very carefully, and then blinked hard. Was it possible? Had she accidentally stumbled on something that could be incredibly important? Then she shook her head. No, she had to be wrong. Things like that just didn't happen.

All the same, there was a small tingle of excitement inside her, and she knew she wanted to check this out. And there was only one way to do that—ask an expert!

She turned down the lamp until it gave off just a dim glow, pulled on a thick, hand-knitted jacket as protection against the chill of the night, and then quietly left the tent.

The obvious person to ask was Peter Wallace. She was just about to make her way over to his tent, when an odd quickening of her pulses made her glance in the opposite direction. She had no idea why—or how—she was picking up these silent signals, but somehow she wasn't surprised to see the tall, dark figure standing about a hundred yards beyond the outer limits of the camp.

For a moment, she hesitated. Max wasn't an expert. He seemed to be fairly knowledgeable about the subject of Egyptology, though, so it might be as well to get his opinion. If he thought the whole thing was crazy nonsense, then at least it would have stopped her from making an absolute fool of herself in front of Peter Wallace.

She hurried over to him. When she was just a few feet away, though, Max turned to confront her, the bright moonlight falling directly on to his face so that she could clearly see the hostility written there.

'There's little enough privacy in this camp at the best of times,' he growled. 'Do you have to follow me out here in the middle of the night? Aren't I allowed half an hour of my own company?'

Ignoring his unexpected blast of temper, Bethan shook her head rather impatiently. 'Never mind that. I've got something to show you.'

'I'm not interested in seeing it—whatever it is,' he added meaningfully.

Her eyes lit up with sudden indignation as the clear import of his words got through to her. 'Do you think I've come chasing after you because I—I——' She couldn't get the words out, they were lost in a furious splutter.

'Why else are you here?'

His drawled challenge took her breath away. The arrogance of the man! The sheer conceit! She was just about to turn and stalk away, but at the last moment she stopped. She needed to talk to someone about the wild idea that was going round and round inside her head, and Max was the ideal person—if he would just stop being so deliberately infuriating for a few minutes!

She held out the book that had been tucked under her arm. 'I was reading this tonight. And Max, something I saw in it made me really sit up and take notice. You see, there was this photo of——'

'Bethan, it's very late,' Max cut in, his voice clearly signalling a total lack of interest in whatever she wanted to tell him. 'Whatever this is all about, it can wait until morning.'

'No, it *can't*,' she insisted impatiently. 'Look, this won't take long—especially if you stop arguing and just listen.'

'Have I got any choice?' he enquired with heavy resignation.

'It doesn't look like it,' she said, more cheerful now she had got his full attention. Before leaving the tent, she had shoved a small torch into the pocket of her jeans. She fished it out, flicked on the thin beam of light, then opened the book and impatiently turned the pages until she found the one she wanted. 'Do you see this?' she said excitedly, shining the torchlight on to the page, so that it was clearly illuminated.

Max moved a little closer, trying to get a better look at it. For just an instant, his body brushed against hers, and she could have sworn his muscles briefly tensed. He drew back again almost immediately, then he gave a brief shrug.

'I've seen that photo many times before. It's a picture of the tomb of Queen Hatshepsut.'

'Yes, I know that,' said Bethan. 'But look where the entrance to the tomb is—half-way up a cliff-face, more than two hundred feet from the ground. And you can't even see it from ground level, because of the way the rock-face bulges outwards.'

'If you've read the text, you'll know that the tomb was only half-finished. They eventually abandoned it, and built the tomb on another site altogether.'

'But that doesn't mean they couldn't have built a tomb for another Egyptian queen—or a Pharoah—in a similar situation.'

Max shook his head. 'Bethan, I haven't the slightest idea what you're getting at,' he said, beginning to sound more than a little exasperated.

'Remember when you rescued me from that cliff-top?'

'I'm not likely to forget it!' he shot back rather acidly.

Bethan wasn't in the least discouraged by his repressive attitude. 'Well, I was sitting up there for several hours before you came,' she went on. 'And there wasn't much to do except sit and stare at the scenery. There was a high cliff opposite, and about half-way up there was a round black patch that looked just like the entrance to a cave.' Her eyes shone with excitement. 'Don't you see? It could be the entrance to a tomb, just like the one they started to build for Queen Hatshe—Hat—oh, whatever her name was!'

To her disappointment, Max seemed singularly unimpressed by her announcement.

'I didn't see any sign of a cave.'

'Of course you didn't,' she said with some exasperation. 'It was night when you climbed that cliff. You couldn't possibly have seen it in the dark.'

'How come you haven't mentioned this before?'

'I'd forgotten about it,' she admitted frankly. 'And even if I'd remembered it, I probably wouldn't have thought it was very significant. It wasn't until I was reading this book and saw the photo that something clicked, and I started putting two and two together.'

'And you've probably come up with five. In fact, there's a good chance you didn't see a cave at all, only a dark patch of shadow. In this sort of harsh, blinding sunlight, your eyes often play tricks on you.'

His total lack of enthusiasm made her want to stamp her foot in sheer frustration. He could at least admit she *might* have stumbled on something important.

'Perhaps we were both hallucinating that day,' she retorted a trifle sulkily. '*I* thought I saw a cave, and *you* thought you saw the ghost of Nefertiti.'

The moonlight was bright enough for her to see the sudden change that swept over Max's features. It was as if something had suddenly clicked inside his head, releasing memories which he preferred to keep locked away.

'But my ghost turned out to be flesh and blood,' he reminded her, in a voice that had suddenly taken on an unexpectedly husky timbre. 'With beautiful eyes and dark, silken hair——' His voice abruptly broke off, as if he had only just realised what he was saying. Then he shook his head, as if trying to rid himself of a haunting image. 'My God, you tempt me, Bethan,' he went on in a harsher tone. 'And sometimes, I think you know exactly how much.'

The sudden change of mood, of atmosphere, made her nerves prickle. Yet it wasn't an entirely unpleasant sensation.

'I don't do it on purpose,' she said in a small voice.

'Don't you? Perhaps not,' Max conceded, a little thickly. 'But it still keeps happening. I keep telling myself that I must be insane, risking getting involved with a spoilt, stubborn brat like you. But then you look at me with those huge eyes of yours . . .'

Bethan could feel her heart beating in queer, jerky thuds. The book she had been holding fell from her nerveless fingers, but she couldn't bend and pick it up. In fact, she couldn't seem to move at all. And she certainly couldn't back away as Max edged nearer, moving slowly now, as if he were still trying to resist the pull, but was fighting a battle that he had always been doomed to lose.

The kiss that followed seemed inevitable, as if it were the only reason the two of them were here to-night. And when his lips possessed hers, it wasn't gently, but with hard male desire. His tongue thrust forcefully into her soft mouth, and she knew he was aching to possess her entire body in exactly the same way. The knowledge should have shocked her, but

it didn't. Instead, she revelled in that endless,
exquisite assault on her bruised mouth; she found
herself swaying against Max, feeling the hard
imprint of his body against her own melting bones.

Her arms slid involuntarily around his neck. She
told herself it was to stop herself from falling as all
the strength seemed to drain from her legs. Then
they remained there to savour the outline of
powerful muscles through the thin leather of his
jacket. She didn't ever want to let go.

When Max's mouth finally left hers, her small
sound of protest turned into a sigh of pleasure as he
bent his head and greedily sought the delicate skin of
her neck and throat, leaving a trail of scorched,
bruised skin behind as his lips selfishly took what
they so desired.

'Like rich honey,' he murmured in an unsteady
voice as his tongue lapped against the soft silk of her
skin.

The moon seemed to be spiralling above them
now, a pale blur of front of Bethan's unfocused eyes.
Nothing was real, nothing had any substance. Her
mind, her body, could concentrate on nothing
except this crazy, delicious slide into a whirlpool of
sheer, unashamed sensuality. And the thundering of
Max's heart against her outspread palm was vivid
proof that he was caught up in the same storm of
insanity.

Then it went dark again as he moved closer,
blotting out the moonlight. He was enveloping her
now in the heat of his own body, locking her tightly
against him, matching his own fierce arousal against
her own slower, more timid response. Bethan
shivered. It was a little piece of paradise, a little
piece of hell, mixed together in a heart-stopping

mixture.

His hands slid the jacket from her shoulders; then, with growing impatience, he turned his attention to her blouse. Bethan closed her eyes dizzily as the buttons were torn apart. The cool night air brushed her skin, swiftly followed by the shocking contrast of his heated fingers.

As the blouse swung open, she heard his groan of unconcealed delight as he discovered nothing except the unrestricted warmth of her skin pressing eagerly against his palms. She had got into the habit of not wearing a bra. It was far more comfortable during the heat of the day, and although her breasts were full, they certainly didn't need any support. With no more barriers to hinder him, he swooped in and ruthlessly took advantage of what he had found. In just seconds, Bethan was shuddering deeply as her nipples hardened to two throbbing points that seemed to be on the verge of exploding with pleasure under his fierce caresses. Then a different, more intense quiver of excitement shot through her as his hand moved still lower, gliding in expert circles over her flat stomach. He was deliberately leading her on now, taking her step by pleasure-drenched step, to the point where she couldn't refuse him anything, would willingly give him absolutely everything he desired . . .

And when he had taken what he wanted, he would go back to Caroline.

That thought exploded inside her head without warning, making her head jerk back in pure shock. The effect was traumatic. In just a few seconds, every spark of desire fled from her body. And in its place was a cold, empty ache, and a growing sense of anger and humiliation. What was she *doing?* This man belonged to someone else. At most, she would only ever be second-best. And right now, he was just using her. She was nothing more than a temporary substitute for his absent fiancée—a stand-in!

Aware that she had gone quite rigid, Max raised his head. Then he stared down at her with overbright eyes, their glittering force reflecting the inner turbulence that still shook him.

'What is it?' he muttered.

'If all you want is sex, you should go home to your fiancée!' she hissed at him.

For a moment, she thought he was going to lose his temper. Instinctively, she flinched. Somehow, though, he held on to his self-control. Then she watched edgily as his mouth set into a grim line.

'Caroline and I don't sleep together.' The grated admission almost seemed to be forced out of him. It was as if he deeply resented having to tell her something so personal, but at the same time couldn't stop himself from saying it.

'Why not?' she flung at him recklessly. 'Don't you turn her on?'

He looked as if he badly wanted to hit her. Staunchly, though, Bethan stood her ground. He wasn't going to physically intimidate her!

'She prefers to wait until after the wedding,' Max growled.

As far as Bethan was concerned, his confession certainly explained a lot. His restlessness, those bright, hungry eyes—and the fact that he was willing to spend a lot of time away from his fiancée. A man like Max must find it very frustrating to be engaged to a girl who didn't want to jump straight into bed with him. Well, he certainly wasn't going to work those frustrations off on her!

'Perhaps you had better find yourself a fiancée who shares *all* your interests,' she told him coldly.

Before he had a chance to grate back a reply, she turned round and quickly walked away from him. Terrified that he might follow her, might try to stop her—and equally fearful that she might just weaken and give in to him—she ran the last few yards. Then she dived breathlessly into the safety of the tent she shared with Poppy.

She crashed around noisily for a few moments in the semi-darkness. Poppy only stirred briefly, though, before going back to sleep again. Bethan released a sigh of relief. She got on well with Poppy, but she certainly didn't want to have to explain why she had come charging in late at night in such an agitated state.

She quickly undressed and crawled into bed. Her limbs were still trembling violently, and she was furiously angry with Max at the way he had so callously used her. She managed to convince herself that the whole thing had been pre-planned and then coldly executed. She conveniently forgot that she had approached him in the first instance, that there had been moments when he was so on fire that all that cool self-control had cracked, turning into nothing but a shattered memory.

He would pay for it! she vowed to herself vehemently. One way or another, she would find some means of getting her own back.

She closed her eyes, forced herself to ignore the odd, unfamiliar ache deep in the pit of her stomach, and eventually managed to snatch a couple of hours of disturbed, dream-plagued sleep.

In the morning, she didn't want to leave the tent.

She knew she was acting like a total coward, but she couldn't seem to do anything about it. Her angry, defiant mood of last night had completely vanished. All she was aware of was an overwhelming desire never to see Max Lansdelle ever again.

Eventually, she gave a deep sigh, swung herself off the bed, and reluctantly began to wash and dress. She couldn't seem to stop thinking about what had happened last night, though. She brushed her hair, and found herself remembering how it had felt as Max had run his fingers through its heavy thickness. As she pulled on a cotton blouse, the thin material rubbed against her breasts, making her realise that they still felt a little sore, a little tender.

Oh, stop it! she lectured herself impatiently. Do you suppose he gave you more than a passing thought after you left him last night? Well, just return the compliment by forgetting that he ever laid a hand on you!

With new determination, she marched out of the tent. After a quick glance around, she found that only Poppy and Steve were still in camp, and they were just leaving. Poppy waved, then she and Steve ambled off to the new excavation site, obviously intending to put in a couple of hours' work before the sun's heat became too fierce.

Bethan made herself some coffee. It was strong and reviving, but she had only drunk half a mugful when a shadow fell over her.

'Any coffee to spare?' asked a familiar voice.

She nearly choked on the mouthful she had just swallowed. A strong hand thumped her helpfully on the back. When she had finally finished spluttering, she glared at Max balefully.

'You've got a nerve! Strolling over here as if—as

if——'

'As if nothing had happened?' Max finished helpfully. He sat down opposite her. 'But what's the alternative?' he questioned in an infuriatingly calm voice. 'This is a very small camp. We can hardly avoid one another indefinitely. Unless you're planning on returning to England, we're going to see each other virtually every day. And I shouldn't think you've got any intention of leaving, even though your holiday must be up by now. You're more likely to stick around just to annoy me!'

'The fact that I'm staying doesn't have anything to do with you,' she retorted. 'I'm here because I want to be a part of what's going on. It's exciting.'

'No, it isn't,' Max responded coolly. 'At the moment, it's extremely boring. It'll only be exciting if Peter ever finds that elusive tomb. And it's beginning to look less and less likely that he's going to do that.'

'But there's always a chance,' Bethan insisted. 'That's why I intend to stay put.'

'Then we'd better lay down a few ground rules. That way, we might be able to avoid another situation like last night.'

The colour began to rise in her face. 'You're the one who seems to be having problems in that direction! Just keep away from me, and everything will be fine.'

His amber eyes briefly gleamed. 'But that's the main difficulty. I don't *want* to stay away from you.'

'If you're that desperate for female company, I dare say there are plenty of girls in Luxor who'll keep you company for the night. I'm sure you can afford the best!' she added with deliberate insult.

Max didn't rise to the bait. In fact, he seemed

determined to keep everything very low-key this morning.

'You weren't listening to what I was saying. I told you that I didn't want to stay away from *you.*'

Their gazes briefly locked for a moment, and an inner shiver ran through Bethan's raw nerves. Her mind was suddenly flooded with vivid memories: the sensation of that hard body crushed against hers, curve matching curve, hot skin burning through thin layers of clothing as if they didn't even exist. And Max's lips seeking out the soft, vulnerable places and then ruthlessly branding them with his own highly distinctive kisses.

Then her head cleared, and reality rushed back in.

'There's one little thing you forgot to mention,' she said in a hard voice. 'Where does your fiancée fit into all this?'

Max drew in a sharp breath. With some satisfaction, Bethan realised that her blunt words had struck home.

'I don't intend to discuss Caroline with you,' he said tautly at last.

'Why not? You're not ashamed of her, are you? I thought she was exactly what you wanted. The ideal wife for a merchant banker.'

'Yes—she would be.'

Yet there was an uncharacteristic note of uncertainty in his voice. He sounded like a man who, perhaps for the first time in his life, was unsure of himself. Who was beginning to wonder if he had made the right decision. And he wouldn't like being in that sort of situation. Oh, no, Bethan thought to herself. He wouldn't like it at all!

But, on the other hand, he had given no indication that he was about to change his mind. And there was no place for her in his life while Caroline still had a claim on him.

'The way I see it, we can either have a platonic relationship—or no relationship at all, she told him firmly. 'I don't mean that we can't spend time together,' she added, looking straight at him. 'I'm quite willing for us to be friends. That's as far as it goes, though. Lay one single finger on me—and you'll be very sorry.'

To her amazement, he accepted her ultimatum without anger or argument. In fact, he seemed almost relieved by her blunt statement, as if it had taken the pressure off him.

'Under the circumstances, it seems the best solution,' he agreed. 'By the way,' he went on, after a short pause, 'you dropped this last night.'

He handed her the book which had fallen from her nerveless fingers when he had first moved towards her to kiss her. Bethan stared at it for a few moments. Then she forced herself to take it.

'Thank you,' she said in a subdued voice.

'I had another look at it this morning. Are you absolutely certain you saw that cave?'

'Yes,' she said, without hesitation.

'Then I suppose it wouldn't hurt to take a look at it. I haven't anything else on this morning, and it won't take more than an hour or so. I'll let you know what I find.'

Instantly, her head shot up. 'If you're going, then I'm coming with you,' she said firmly.

'I don't think that would be a very good idea.'

'Why not?' she challenged. Then, seeing the dark expression which flashed across his face, she went on, 'Look, Max, this doesn't have anything to do

with any—well, any problems we might have had
last night. That's *my* cave. And if you're going to
find anything, then I want to be there.'

'My God, you're stubborn!' he said with some
feeling.

She gave a brief grin. 'I told you before, I've spent
most of my life getting exactly what I wanted. It's a
hard habit to break. So, are you going to take me
with you?'

Max gave a resigned shrug. 'If I refused, you'd
probably just run along behind the Land Rover! All
right—get yourself ready. We'll leave in about ten
minutes.'

As Bethan went to find a large floppy hat to
protect her head from the sun, and a pair of sun-
glasses, it rather belatedly occurred to her that this
wasn't the most sensible thing she had ever
done—throwing herself straight back into Max's
company only a few hours after their turbulent
encounter last night.

You've got to get used to being around him, she
excused herself. He isn't just going to go away. And
there shouldn't be any problems now you've got
everything straightened out. He's more or less
agreed not to touch you, and he's a man who keeps
his word.

Several minutes later, she was scrambling into the
Land Rover. At the last moment, she had changed
her shorts for a pair of cotton jeans. She already felt
rather hot in them, but she had decided that it might
not be a good idea to flash her bare legs around.
There was no point in asking for trouble.

The Land Rover bumped its way over the rough
floor of the valley. Soon, the camp site had
disappeared from view, and after a while they were

trundling along another valley, which was rather narrower. Bethan glanced up, then realised that she recognised the high cliff on her right. She could even see the patch of scree where she had slipped and wrenched her knee.

'Did I really climb that?' she said, with a grimace. 'I must have been mad!'

'It probably wasn't the cleverest thing you've done,' agreed Max. He brought the Land Rover to a halt, and then got out. 'You think the cave is in the cliff opposite?'

'Yes. About half-way up.' She screwed up her eyes against the strong light, and studied the cliff carefully. Finally, though, she shook her head. 'I don't think it can be seen from ground level. See that overhang?' She pointed to a section of the cliff which bulged outwards. 'I'm sure it's just above that.'

Max looked at the cliff-face assessingly. 'It's climbable,' he said at last. 'But I can't manage that overhang without the proper equipment.' He paused for a moment, then added, 'But I could climb slightly to the right, and then work my way across.'

The cliffs on this side of the valley were far more steep than on the other side, where Bethan had clambered up without too much difficulty. She studied his proposed route, and then promptly shook her head.

'It's too dangerous.

'Merchant bankers like to live dangerously.' His amber eyes glinted. 'Don't you know that we can't resist a challenge?'

Bethan scowled. 'Climb it, then! But don't expect me to pick up the pieces if you fall off.'

'Don't worry, sweetheart. I'll be perfectly safe.' And he began to climb while she was still trying to work out if that endearment had been delivered in a mocking tone or not.

Max climbed easily and confidently, and seemed to know exactly what he was doing. All the same, the sweat inched its way down Bethan's spine as she watched him. She was hot, that was all, she told herself rather crossly. She certainly wasn't worried about his safety.

He soon reached the section where the rock-face began to bulge outwards. Moving more slowly now, he edged his way round to the right, and then eased himself across to the overhang. The sun glinted briefly on his dark hair. Then he moved a few more feet, and suddenly disappeared from sight.

Bethan blinked a couple of times, wondering if her eyes were playing tricks on her. It was as if the cliff had just swallowed him up. For a few moments, she felt alarmingly close to panic. Then she finally realised what had happened. There *was* a cave up there—and Max was now inside it.

Excitement immediately took the place of fear. What would he find? Just a musty old cave, or——? Her imagination seized up at that point. She couldn't imagine what it would be like to find a lost tomb of one of the pharaohs.

It seemed ages before Max reappeared. She was just beginning to get worried again, imagining all sorts of awful accidents. And she was stuck down here, on the ground. If he was in trouble, she wouldn't be able to do a thing to help him.

Then he came back into sight, easing himself out on to the cliff-face. Bethan released an enormous sigh of relief. He climbed down at a speed which seemed, to her, quite recklessly fast. As soon as his feet touched the ground, she dashed over to him.

'Well?' she demanded. 'What did you find? Max—what's *there*?'

'There *is* a cave,' he told her, obviously amused at her bursting excitement. 'And once you're inside it, there's a tunnel which seems to run quite a long way back into the cliff.'

'And is there a tomb?'

'I've no idea. I couldn't get very far. Part of the roof has collapsed, completely blocking the tunnel.'

'Oh,' she said gloomily. 'Then that's it?'

'Not necessarily. I don't think the rock-fall would be too difficult to clear. Then we could find out if anything lies behind it.'

Her eyes instantly brightened again. 'How soon can we start?'

Max held up one hand warningly. 'Before we go any further, I think we ought to bring Peter in on this. He is in charge of this expedition.'

'But it's my cave,' she insisted stubbornly. 'I found it.'

'If you like, I'll chisel your name over the entrance,' came his slightly exasperated response. 'Then no one will ever be able to forget that fact!'

She flushed slightly. 'It's just that I've never found anything important before.'

'And you might not have found anything this time,' he reminded her crushingly. 'There's probably nothing up there except a long, empty tunnel. And even if by some million to one chance there *is* something significant in that cave, we can't go charging in there like a demolition gang. This is an archaeological expedition, remember? Everything has to be carefully photographed and recorded every step of the way.'

'I suppose you're right,' she said rather grudgingly. Then she brightened up again. 'When can we begin?'

'First things first. We'll tell Peter, and then we'll make out a list of the equipment we'll need. Quite apart from anything else, there's the problem of how to get up to that cave. I'm probably the only one in camp who can manage that climb.'

Bethan hadn't thought of that. 'How about a rope-ladder?' she suggested.

'That might work,' Max agreed. He nodded towards the Land Rover. 'Let's get back to camp. We can't do much else here.'

Once back at camp, though, Bethan's enthusiam was immediately dampened by the discovery that Peter had gone to Luxor, and probably wouldn't be back until much later that day.

'That's it, then,' shrugged Max. 'We can't do anything until Peter returns.'

'Oh, how can you *bear* to wait?' she grumbled. 'Can't we just go ahead without him?'

His amber gaze instantly fixed on her sternly. 'No, we can't. Peter's been working on this project for more than five years. I'm not going to cut him out just when it looks as if there might be a chance of finding something.'

Bethan shot him a sheepish look. 'I suppose I'm being totally selfish again.'

'Yes,' he said without compunction. Then he relented a fraction. 'But at least you're ready to admit it. That's got to be a point in your favour.'

She gave a rueful sigh. 'Has it? Sometimes I think I'm not making any progress at all. That I'm still the awful brat I was a couple of years ago.' She lifted her head and looked at him. 'Do you mind if I ask you something?' she said a little shyly. 'Do you—well, do you like me?'

A dark expression instantly swept over Max's face. 'That's a rather loaded question,' he growled.

'Not really,' she insisted. 'I just wondered what you actually thought of me. You see, I was such an out and out pain when I was younger that I should think just about everyone had a pretty low opinion of me. I have been trying to improve since then, but it's hard to know exactly how I'm doing. It would be really helpful to have an honest assessment. I don't mean, do you fancy me, or find me attractive,' she rushed on hurriedly, not wanting him to get the wrong idea. 'Just—am I the sort of person you enjoy having around? Do you actually like me?'

Max stared at her so intently that she began to feel thoroughly uncomfortable. What a stupid thing to have asked him, she told herself miserably. Why couldn't she have kept her mouth shut?

He half turned, as if he was about to walk away without answering. At the last moment, though, he swung back and fixed the full force of that disturbing amber gaze on her.

'Yes, I like you,' he said in a low voice. 'Perhaps only the devil knows why—but I do.' Then he quickly strode off, as if already regretting making that admission.

CHAPTER SEVEN

PETER WALLACE returned to the camp just after lunch. Max immediately took him into the main tent, and Bethan hovered impatiently outside, waiting to see what his verdict would be.

Max finally emerged nearly quarter of an hour later. 'He wants to see the cave,' he said with a grin.

The three of them piled into the Land Rover, and Max drove them back to the narrow, barren, sun-filled valley. Peter frowned when he saw the exact position of the cave, and he made no attempt to climb up and see it for himself at close quarters, but Bethan couldn't blame him for that. She wouldn't have tackled that climb, either. It would be all right once Max had fixed a rope-ladder into place.

It was decided that only the three of them would know about it for now. If it turned out to be just an empty cave, then they wouldn't have raised everyone's hopes for nothing. And if, by some fantastic chance, they actually found something, then it would be better if as few people as possible knew about it. That way, they would reduce the risk of looters moving in.

When everyone was gathered together for the main meal the following evening, Peter casually announced that he was declaring the next couple of days a holiday. He turned to Steve and Poppy. 'You've worked hard these last few weeks. Why not take yourselves off to Luxor and book into a hotel for a couple of nights? Enjoy a bit of comfort for a change. I'll cover all your expenses, of course.'

'What will you do while we're away?' asked Poppy.

'Oh—I've one or two new lines of research I want to follow up,' Peter answered, with deliberate vagueness. Then he grinned at her. 'You're not going to turn down the chance of a break, are you?'

'Certainly not!' Poppy said promptly. 'I'll probably spend every minute of it soaking in a hot bath. How about you, Bethan?'

Bethan jumped rather guiltily. She didn't like the thought of deceiving Poppy—even though they hadn't actually told her any outright lies—and she was relieved when Peter answered for her.

'Bethan's volunteered to stay here and cook our meals.'

'Men!' said Poppy in exasperation. 'You're all such helpless babies. Can't you get your own meals for a couple of days?'

'I don't mind staying,' Bethan assured her hurriedly. Then she gave an inward groan as she saw the comprehending expression that spread over Poppy's face. Poppy looked from Bethan to Max, and then back again. Finally, she gave a knowing nod and a mere hint of a wink. It was pretty obvious what was going through Poppy's head. She thought that it was Max Lansdelle's charms that had persuaded Bethan to remain behind at the camp. To Bethan's relief, though, Poppy refrained from any sly comments or outright teasing.

Early next morning, Poppy and Steve left for Luxor. Ahmed, and the couple of other Egyptians who helped out with the manual labour involved in the dig, had already returned to their village. Only

Max, Peter and Bethan were left at the camp now. They loaded the Land Rover with the equipment that Peter had brought from Luxor yesterday afternoon, and then the three of them jumped in and drove back to the site of the cave.

Before anything else could be done, Max had to climb up and fix the rope-ladder in place. Bethan glanced up rather nervously at the cliff. It seemed even steeper than it had been yesterday.

'Be careful,' she said to Max a little edgily.

He grinned back at her. 'Bankers only take acceptable risks.' Then he fixed a thin coil of rope around his shoulders, and began to climb.

Familiar now with the foot and hand-holds, it took him less time than before. In just minutes, he reached the overhang; then he uncoiled the rope around his shoulder and let it snake down to the ground. Peter tied the end to the rope-ladder, and Max hauled it up. It took him a while to hammer stout pegs into the rock to secure the ladder, but finally it was in place.

Bethan turned to Peter. 'You can go up now,' she said, rather enviously.

There had been a fierce argument earlier, which she had finally lost. Max had been adamant. He and Peter would climb up to the cave and do a preliminary survey, while she stayed on the ground.

'You're leaving me behind because I'm female!' she had accused.

'You're absolutely right,' Max had agreed calmly. Then his tone had altered. 'Any more arguments about this, Bethan, and I'll send you to join Poppy and Steve in Luxor.'

Knowing that he was quite capable of carrying out his threat, she had subsided into a rather sulky silence.

Now she waited for Peter to climb the ladder. He seemed to be dithering about, though, instead of going straight up.

'Go on,' she said encouragingly. 'I'll hold it steady for you.'

He turned to face her, and to her surprise, she saw he had gone awfully white. 'I don't think I can do it,' he said unsteadily.

'Why ever not?'

'I can't stand heights,' Peter confessed, rather sheepishly. 'I was hoping I'd be able to make it—I'd give just about anything to see the inside of that cave—but look at me.' He held out his hands, which were visibly trembling. 'Just the thought of going up that ladder is giving me the shakes.'

'Well, if you can't make it, then I'll have to go,' Bethan said, her eyes suddenly gleaming with anticipation.

'I'm not sure that's a good idea.' Peter said doubtfully. 'Max didn't want you up there.'

'He won't be able to do much about it once I'm actually there!' She put one foot on the ladder, determined to go ahead before Peter could think up any objections. 'See you later, Peter.'

The climb was more exhausting than she had thought it would be, and definitely more nerve-racking. As she went higher and higher, the ladder creaked and swayed, and she could feel her heart beginning to pound. Her legs felt rather shaky, too, but she wasn't sure if it was from the exertion of the climb, or the thought of what Max was going to say when her head popped over the top.

With a gasp of relief, she finally reached the overhang. She hauled herself off the ladder, then rolled

on to the small, flat area of rock in front of the cave.
Strong hands were holding her and steadying
her—Max's hands, she realised, with a nervous
thump of her pulses. Raising her head, she gazed up
at him rather defiantly. She *wasn't* going to be
intimidated by the angry blaze in those amber eyes.

'What are you doing here? Where's Peter?' he demanded curtly.

'He couldn't make it up the ladder. He's afraid of
heights.'

'He's *what*?'

'Afraid of heights,' she repeated patiently.

'Why the hell didn't he tell me?'

'He was probably embarrassed. Men hate having
to admit to weakness—any weakness.'

Max's gaze bored down into her, but he didn't
say anything.

'Anyway, he was hoping he'd be able to manage
it,' Bethan chattered on nervously. 'When it came
down to it, though, he couldn't. So I came instead.'

'And you can just go straight down again,' he
growled.

'Oh, no,' she said immediately. 'Now I'm here,
I'm staying. And I don't think you can do much
about it,' she added with a more cheerful grin.
'Short of chucking me over the edge, of course.'

'Don't think I'm not tempted!'

He aimed another furious glare at her, and looked
as if he would like to say a lot more on the subject.
Rather to her surprise, though, he then turned away
and began to haul up a canvas sling, which held the
equipment they might be needing. Bethan held her
breath. Was that it? Was he going to let her stay?
She tensely waited for a couple more minutes, and
then gradually started to relax. It looked as if

she had got away with it! He had accepted her presence here as a *fait accompli*.

While Max sorted through the equipment, Bethan took a closer look at the entrance to the cave. Wide at the mouth, and then narrowing slightly as it turned into a tunnel that led back into the shadowy depths of the cliff, it seemed both mysterious and a little frightening. She went to step inside, but then hesitated. She wasn't scared—of course she wasn't. But on the other hand, it probably wouldn't hurt to wait for Max.

'We'll leave everything here for now, except for the torches,' Max decided. 'There's no point in carrying a lot of stuff that we might not even need.' He handed her a torch, and then picked up the other one. 'Ready?'

She nodded. 'Er—you go first,' she said generously.

Max grinned, as if he knew perfectly well that she was too nervous to take the lead. Then he stepped inside the cave.

The dark shadows quickly closed in on them, and Bethan was very glad that the torches had powerful beams.

'This place is eerie,' she whispered in a voice that seemed to echo right back to her.

'Don't spook yourself,' advised Max. 'Do that, and you'll start seeing the ghosts of long-dead Pharaohs gliding out of the walls.'

'Are you trying to scare me?' she demanded.

Her voice came out even edgier than she had expected. Max shot a quick glance at her, then silently held out his hand.

After only a moment's hesitation, she took it. As soon as his fingers closed firmly around her own, she felt much better. In a place like this, it was definitely comforting to have warm, physical contact with another human being.

'How far is it to the spot where the roof's collapsed?' asked Bethan, instinctively keeping her voice low.

'Only a few more yards. The tunnel winds round to the right just ahead. Then we'll be at the place where it's blocked.'

Despite the hot, dry air in the tunnel, small goose-pimples of excitement raced over Bethan's skin. What if there *were* something on the other side of that rock-fall?

'Poor Peter,' she said sympathetically. 'He must be absolutely sick, having to miss out on this.'

'I'm not too thrilled about it, either,' commented Max. 'I'd much prefer to have him with me, instead of you.'

'Charming! Do I bore you that much?'

'I don't think that "bored" is quite the word to describe the way I feel when you're around,' he replied drily. 'I simply meant this is no sort of situation for a woman to be in.'

'Oh, I get it,' she retorted with some sarcasm. 'Only the men are allowed to take part in any of the exciting bits. I suppose you'd have liked me to have stayed back in the camp, cooking dinner, so you could come back to a hot meal afterward!'

Exasperation flared briefly in his eyes. 'Don't twist my words.'

'Then what *did* you mean?'

'Only that there's always an element of risk in any venture like this. And I don't intend to see you hurt. At the first sign of any danger, you're to get straight out of here.'

'And what if I refuse to go?'

Max's eyes fixed on her until her own gaze faltered, and she was forced to look away.

'You won't refuse,' he told her flatly.

Bethan could see this was one argument she wasn't going to win. Anyway, she didn't want to waste time arguing with Max. She wanted to get on, and see what was at the other end of this tunnel.

They rounded the bend in the tunnel; then Bethan gave a small groan of dismay as she saw the pile of rubble which completely blocked their way.

'We'll never get past that!'

Max shone the torchlight on the rock-fall, assessing it carefully.

'It shouldn't be too difficult to clear,' he said at last. 'It's mostly loose stuff. If I clear a passage at the top, we should be able to crawl through.' He beamed the torchlight upwards, so that it illuminated the roof. 'That looks fairly solid. I don't think any more's going to come down.' Then he looked more closely. 'See those marks?' he said, with a frown.

Bethan peered up. 'It looks as if someone's been hammering away at the rock,' she said, puzzled. 'It's all chipped and gouged.' Then light suddenly dawned. 'You mean that someone *deliberately* brought down part of the roof? It's not an accident that the tunnel's blocked?'

'It looks like it,' agreed Max.

'But—why would anyone do that?'

'Perhaps because there's something at the end of this tunnel that they wanted to keep well hidden.' Then, seeing the bright excitement in her eyes, he warned, 'I could be wrong. We won't know until we're on the other side of that rock-fall.' He caught hold of her by the shoulders and pushed her a few yards back along the tunnel. 'Stay there while I shift some of this rubble,' he instructed.

'Why can't I help?'

'Because if any more of that roof *does* come down, I'd rather it fell on my head and not yours.'

'What about equality of the sexes?' she demanded.

'We'll be as equal as you like, once we're out of this tunnel,' Max said, quite unperturbed. 'Right now, you'll do exactly as I say—or you won't like the consequences. If you want to do something useful, shine the torchlight directly on to the rock-fall, so I can see what I'm doing.'

Although she was still muttering rebelliously under her breath, Bethan obeyed. Max began to shift the stones with ease, clearing a small gap at the top of the pile of rubble in a very short time.

'Hand me one of the torches,' he ordered. After Bethan had passed one over, he shone it through the gap.

'What can you see?' she asked eagerly.

'Take a look for yourself.'

She scrambled up beside him, then aimed the beam of the torch through the hole. 'It's just a continuation of the tunnel,' she said at last, in a disappointed voice.

Max nodded. 'No tomb entrance, no wall paintings, no sign of any royal seal—I don't think we're going to find anything, Bethan.'

'You mean, you're going to give up?'

'We've come this far—I suppose we might as well see it through to the end,' he decided, after a brief pause.

'Good,' she said, with some satisfaction. 'I knew

you weren't a quitter.'

'You mean that I never give up until I get what I want?' His mouth curled into a gently mocking smile. 'That can be a rather dangerous quality in a man.'

Suddenly aware that she was wedged uncomfortably close against Max—that their faces were still only inches apart, where they had drawn together to peer through the gap—she hurriedly slithered away from him.

'Can you make a big enough hole for us to get through?'

'I don't see why not. This stuff is fairly easy to shift.'

Quarter of an hour later, Max had cleared a sizeable hole in the rubble. He had stripped off to the waist now, and the sweat glistened on his skin as he worked steadily on in the musty heat that had built up inside the tunnel. For a banker, he certainly had very powerful muscles, Bethan told herself wryly. And he definitely hadn't developed them sitting behind a desk! But then, she already knew he enjoyed rock-climbing. She wouldn't mind betting that most of his other hobbies and interests were physical, too. He was a man who would need to balance the intellectual demands of his job with outlets for the pent-up energy that would build up during working hours, demanding release during his free time.

She enjoyed watching him handling the solid chunks of rock as easily as if they had been made of polystyrene. There was a rhythm to his movements which was quite absorbing; she could have sat and watched him all day.

Then he paused for a few moments, to study the progress he had made so far. The torchlight shone

on the bronzed outline of his body, and the dark hair
which was now sticking damply to the nape of his
neck. He seemed unaware of her scrutiny; yet,
before turning back to his task again, he lifted his
head and shot a brief, unexpected smile in her
direction.

That smile seemed to hit her straight in the middle
of the solar plexus. She wasn't even sure that she
hadn't gasped out loud. Max had already begun
shifting more rocks again, now, so he didn't catch
her reaction. Bethan was numbly grateful for that
because she was suddenly caught up in a storm of
confusion.

As her head slowly cleared, she blinked in
astonishment. Just one smile—and she felt as if she
had fallen off a cliff! Crazy, she told herself shakily.
And a little scary, too, because it was pretty obvious
what it meant. Why hadn't she seen it before,
though? It would have given her time to back off,
perhaps even run away. She gave a ragged sigh.
Whichever way she looked at it, this certainly wasn't
a very convenient moment to realise that she was
tumbling headlong into love with Max Lansdelle!

He belongs to someone else, she reminded herself
fiercely. A cool, beautiful blonde called Caroline.
And even if he were free, she still wouldn't be in
with much of a chance. Most of the time, Max let his
head very firmly rule his heart. He wanted a
'suitable' wife—and that was what he was obviously
determined to have. Whichever way she looked at it,
Bethan couldn't see herself ever fitting into that
category.

She closed her eyes, suddenly wishing that she
was miles away from here. She couldn't get excited
about this tunnel any longer, not even if Aladin's

cave lay at the end of it. The bright sparkle seemed to have gone right out of the day. All she really wanted at the moment was some time to herself, to get used to the idea that she had done something catastrophically stupid.

'Are you all right?'

Max's voice broke sharply into her turbulent thoughts. Quickly, she opened her eyes again. Just the sight of him sent her pulses racing. She must have been blind not to have realised what was happening to her.

'I'm—I'm fine,' she somehow managed to get out. 'It's just rather stuffy in here. I feel—a bit woozy.'

Which was definitely an understatement! If she stood up right now, she was sure she would topple right over. She couldn't remember her legs ever feeling so hopelessly weak before.

'Do you want to go back to the cave entrance?' asked Max, with a frown. 'You can get some fresh air while I take a look down the tunnel.'

That revived her a little. 'You've cleared the rock-fall? We can get through? Then I'm coming with you,' she said, with a fresh surge of resolution.

'Are you sure you're up to it? You don't look too good.'

Bethan forced back the wild desire to giggle. Should she tell him the truth? That she was suffering from a sudden attack of love? Better not, she decided. It probably wouldn't go down at all well!

She got to her feet, and was relieved to find her rubbery legs would just about hold her up.

'Lead on,' she said, with a weak grin. 'And don't worry—I'll be close behind you every step of the way.'

'I dare say you will,' Max remarked drily. 'You're a very difficult girl to shake off—in every sense of the word.'

And while she was still trying to work out what he meant by that, he picked up one of the torches and disappeared through the gap in the rock-fall.

Bethan scrambled after him, wrinkling her nose as they began to make their way along the tunnel on the other side.

'I wish someone had installed air-conditioning!'

'It's quite breathable. It's just very stale,' said Max.

'How far do you suppose this tunnel goes?'

'I've no idea. I haven't got second sight.'

She shut up after that, and instead concentrated on not stumbling as the ground under their feet became more uneven. The tunnel twisted a couple of times and then, just as Bethan was wishing she had listened to Max's advice and gone back to the cave entrance, it started to widen.

The beams of light from the torches danced on ahead of them, revealing that the roof had begun to soar way above their heads. Bethan realised they were entering a large cavern. As they walked further inside, the torchlight began to reflect a dull glow, as if the floor had suddenly changed colour. It didn't seem to be solid rock any longer; she had the vivid impression it was covered with . . .

'Gold!' breathed Bethan, stopping dead with sheer disbelief. She rubbed her eyes, but it didn't make any difference—the gold glow didn't fade. 'Max, I think you'd better pinch me—and hard! I'm starting to hallucinate.'

'Either we're sharing the same hallucination or we're actually seeing this,' Max answered drily. He took a couple of steps forward, then bent down and picked up a small gold statuette. 'It's real enough. It looks as if we've just hit the jackpot!'

Bethan shone the torch around the cavern, exclaiming softly under her breath as the powerful beam of light picked out and illuminated the treasures which were so carelessly scattered all over the ground. The glint of gold seemed to be everywhere; gold, and the bright sparkle of precious stones.

Her dazzled eyes began to make out individual items. Small statues of gods and goddesses, some with rather grotesque animal heads. Jewellery—magnificent jewellery, which Bethan hankered to pick up and try on, to wear for just a few marvellous moments. Rings and bracelets, gold collars, exquisite ear-rings, studded with lapis lazuli, turquoise, carnelian; so many gemstones, all glittering in the light. Then there were the handsome daggers, caskets covered with the finest filigree work, alabaster vases embellished with gold and ivory. Everywhere she looked, her stunned gaze fell on items of the finest craftsmanship. The cave shimmered with the brilliance of a priceless treasure from an ancient civilisation.

Max was the first to recover his wits. He carefully replaced the statue he had picked up, and then straightened up again.

'We'd better not touch or move anything. Sorting through all this is going to be a job for the experts.'

'But where did all this come from?' asked Bethan, her voice still dazed. 'This isn't a tomb, is it?'

'No, it's not.' His dark brows drew together. 'My guess is that this is the cache of a tomb-robber,' he said at last. 'And probably not a modern robber.

This stuff could well have been here for centuries.'

'You mean that someone looted one of the tombs of the Pharaohs, and then hid everything here for safety?'

'It's the most likely explanation,' said Max. 'The looter must have thought he'd found the perfect hiding-place—which he had. He even engineered that rock-fall in the tunnel, to help safeguard his hoard of treasure.' He frowned. 'Something must have happened to prevent him from coming back to collect it. Most likely, he died. And probably fairly suddenly—perhaps even violently—since he obviously didn't get a chance to tell anyone where he'd hidden the loot.'

Bethan gave a small shiver. 'Do you think you can save the gory details until we're out of here?'

'Sorry,' grinned Max. 'I didn't take you for the squeamish type.'

'Normally, I'm not. But there's something about this place that's beginning to give me the creeps,' she admitted. 'I know I wanted to come with you, and it's thrilling to find all this treasure—but I don't think I want to stick around here for too long. There's a funny sort of atmosphere in here.'

'Then let's go back to the cave entrance,' said Max, at once. 'You can wait there, while I come back with one of the cameras and get some photos.'

Bethan took one last look round. 'I suppose I couldn't take a small souvenir back with me?' she said hopefully. 'A gold ring? A nice bracelet dripping with gems? Or perhaps they wouldn't miss one of those rather attractive gold armbands?'

Max raised one eyebrow. 'I don't think that would go down too well! Come on, let's get moving——'

The rest of his words were drowned out by a low, ominous rumble. The very ground they were standing on seemed to shake, and Bethan thought she heard the faint musical chimes of gold rattling against gold. Then clouds of dust began to billow into the cavern. Seconds later, she started to choke as she breathed it down her nose and throat.

An instant later, Max shoved her to the ground with bruising force. Then his hard body dived on top of her, covering her like a living shield. Something was thrown over her head, stopping some of that choking dust from getting into her lungs. Then an eternity seemed to pass before the rumbling gradually ceased and the ground became still again.

Terrified, confused and half-suffocated, Bethan thought the roof of the cavern had collapsed on top of them, that the weight she could feel crushing her into the hard, uneven floor was a heap of rubble, burying her alive. As the first wild rush of panic eased a little, though, she could feel warm skin pressed against her own, the harder outline of human bones, and the harsh breathing of someone whose face was pressed tightly against the nape of her neck. Gradually, she remembered how Max had thrown her to the ground and flung himself over her. With a sigh of relief, she realised it was his body pinning her down, that they hadn't been buried alive.

She tore the folds of cloth from her face. Then she calmed down even more as she realised it was Max's shirt. He must have whipped it off and flung it over her, to try and protect her from that lethal dust.

The air was still thick, but at least it was breathable. And Bethan muttered a small prayer of gratitude when she saw one of the torches was still working.

Then a wave of fresh panic swept over her when she realised Max wasn't moving. He was still sprawled out on top of her, his heavy weight practically crushing her.

Terrified that he might have been badly injured, she gasped out his name. Then she sagged with relief when he slowly stirred, lifting his face from the dusty swirl of her hair, and then sneezing violently several times.

'Are you all right?' he asked, brushing dust from his face and hair.

'I think so,' she answered shakily. 'How about you?'

'Just a few bruises, that's all. Sorry I nearly flattened you, but I thought it was probably better than being knocked out by falling rocks.'

Bethan glanced at the walls and roof of the cavern. 'Nothing seems to have collapsed in here. So, what was all that noise? Where did all the dust come from?'

Max seemed reluctant to answer her question. At last, though, he lifted his head and met her gaze. 'I think that a section of roof in the tunnel must have collapsed,' he said steadily. 'And if I'm right, it means we're in serious trouble.'

She looked at him edgily. 'How serious?'

'We won't know until we take a look. Is only one torch working?'

She picked up the other one. 'I'm afraid so. I dropped this one when all the commotion began. It looks as if the bulb's smashed.' Her lower lip began to quiver. 'I'm sorry,' she muttered in a small voice.

'It wasn't your fault,' Max said in an unexpectedly gentle tone. Then he got to his feet and pulled on his shirt. 'Let's go and take a look at that tunnel, see how bad things are.'

They walked very slowly, with Max shining the torch upwards all the time, studying the roof for any signs of a second cave-in. Everything seemed to have settled down again now, though. Nothing moved except the dust, which was still swirling slowly round, making them cough.

Just past the first bend, though, they found they couldn't go any further. The roof had fallen in, completely blocking the tunnel. Max studied the scene grimly, and Bethan could tell from his face that things were bad.

'We're not going to get out of here, are we?' she said in a voice that was audibly shaking.

'Not without some help from outside,' Max replied, rather grimly. 'If we try and dig our way out there's a good chance we'll bring another chunk of roof down on our head.'

She swallowed hard. 'How long do you think it'll be before any rescuers get here?'

'It shouldn't be too long.'

'You're not saying that just to make me feel better? After all, Peter doesn't even know there's anything wrong,' she reminded him. 'He's sitting out there, thinking we're having a marvellous time exploring this cave. And instead—instead——' Her voice petered out on a distinctly quavery note, and Max immediately put his arm around her shoulder.

'He'll soon realise something's gone wrong,' he said firmly. 'And then he'll hightail it off for help. We'll be out of here soon, and in one piece. I promise you that, Bethan.'

She gave a dejected shrug. 'You sound awfully convincing. I just wish I could believe you.'

'Have I ever lied to you?'

'I don't know. You might have done.'

Max lifted one eyebrow wryly. 'No one could accuse us of having a relationship based on mutual trust and respect!'

'I didn't think we had a relationship at all,' she mumbled.

'Mmm,' was his non-committal reply. Then he began to gently prod her forward. 'Let's get back to the main cavern. I don't want to hang around here, in case another chunk of roof caves in.'

That made Bethan move fairly promptly. She stumbled along beside Max, and gave a small sigh of relief when they arrived back at the cavern. At least they should be fairly safe here. And Max was right, there was really no need to panic. They just had to sit it out until they were rescued.

Max dragged an old pile of sacking out from one corner, so they had something to sit on.

'Where did this come from?' asked Bethan, grimacing a little as she tried to get comfortable on the coarse material.

'They're probably the sacks which were used to carry all this loot down here,' replied Max.

She immediately wrinkled her nose. 'You mean, they belonged to the tomb-robber?'

'No one's forcing you to sit on them,' Max replied equably.

But, since the hard rock floor looked even more uninviting, Bethan decided she would stay where she was.

Max didn't say anything more for several minutes. When Bethan finally turned her head and looked at him, she saw a brooding darkness had settled over his features.

'What's up?' she asked. 'Are you angry about

something?'

'Too damned right I am!' he growled. 'I'm angry with myself.'

'Why? There wasn't anything you could have done. You couldn't have *stopped* that roof falling in.'

'I could have made sure you weren't here when it happened! I should have sent you back, not let you set foot in this place.'

'Then why didn't you?'

'Because I like having you around,' he muttered, after quite a long pause.

His admission made Bethan blink in astonishment. 'Is that a compliment?'

'If it is, you shouldn't be too pleased about it,' Max told her testily. 'It's the reason you're trapped here, instead of being safely back with Peter.'

'You tried to send me back,' she reminded him. 'But as usual, I was completely pig-headed and wouldn't go. Anyway, I know it's a bit scary, but I'm sure everything will turn out all right,' she added with forced optimism.

She had hardly finished speaking, though, when the light from the remaining torch suddenly gave an ominous flicker.

Bethan gulped, and grabbed hold of Max's hand. His fingers immediately closed around hers in a steadying grip, but this time it only made her feel slightly better.

'It's not—it's not going to go out, is it?' she said in a frightened whisper.

'Even if it does, there's nothing to be scared of,' Max assured her comfortingly.

'Perhaps this isn't a very good time to tell you this, but—I don't like the dark,' she confessed. The torch flickered again, and she visibly jumped. 'I've always been a bit of a coward once the lights go out. It started when I was just a kid. I used to sleep all alone in this huge bedroom at the very top of the house. It had very heavy curtains, and if I woke up in the middle of the night, I couldn't see a single thing. And it was always so silent, because none of the rooms nearby were occupied. It was like being lost and alone in the middle of nowhere!'

'You know exactly where you are right now,' Max soothed her. 'And if you get too jumpy, just hold on to me. I'll be here if you need me.'

It was a comforting thought—even a rather pleasant one. Bethan hurriedly told herself that she shouldn't rush to take advantage of his offer, though. Whenever they got too close, things always seemed to get riotously out of hand. The situation was difficult and dangerous enough as it was, without adding to their problems.

Then, without even a last warning flicker, the torch went out completely. The cavern was instantly plunged into total and terrifying darkness. Without hesitation, Bethan gave a squeak of pure panic, and hurled herself straight into Max's arms.

CHAPTER EIGHT

MAX didn't flinch, even though Bethan had her arms wound so tightly around his neck that she must have been half-suffocating him. He held her in a huge bear-hug, rocking her gently, as if she had been a frightened child.

'It's all right,' he crooned, one hand stroking her hair.

'It's not all right,' Bethan got out in a cracked voice. 'Max, it's *dark*!'

'It can't hurt you. What do you think's going to happen?' he teased softly. 'Bogeymen jumping out at you? Ghosts tweaking your hair?'

She began to feel slightly stupid, and she relaxed her grip on him just a fraction.

'I just don't like it,' she muttered.

'Then keep your eyes closed,' Max advised. 'If you can't actually see the darkness, you'll probably feel better.'

She was sitting awkwardly, with one of her legs twisted under her. As she straightened it out, trying to get more comfortable, there was a soft clank as she kicked one of the gold objects that littered the floor.

'All this treasure,' she said in a quiet voice. 'Yet when it comes down to it, it's completely useless. We can't eat it or drink it, and it can't give us any light. I suppose its only real value is in its beauty—and we can't even see it!'

'You must be feeling better—you've started

philosophising!'

'I think I'm probably just trying to distract myself from the mess we're in,' Bethan said glumly.

'Mmm. Come to think of it, I could do with one or two distractions right now. My mind—and certain other parts of me—seem to be fixed on just one thing. This is hardly the time or the place, but they don't seem to know that,' he told her drily. 'And I don't think things are going to improve unless you shift away from me a little.'

'Oh!' came Bethan's flustered response. Right then, she was glad of the darkness because it hid the surge of colour that rushed into her face. She began to disentangle herself from the comforting warmth of his body, but just then there was another faint rumble from the tunnel.

With a frightened gasp, she shot back into his arms again. Max gave a resigned sigh. 'All right, stay where you are for a while longer. I suppose I can stand it for a few more minutes, provided you don't wriggle around too much.'

She remained as still as a statue, willing to do anything as long as it meant she didn't have to move. She could feel the steady thump of Max's heart, and it was marvellously soothing, that slow, rhythmic beat. In spite of everything that had happened, she began to feel curiously relaxed. She didn't even mind the dark so much any more. Max was here, and that made everything all right.

It was quite a while before her senses began to register subtle changes in the hard body that was giving her so much comfort. The even heartbeat began to quicken, and suddenly wasn't quite so steady. She could feel Max breathing rather faster, and he shifted restlessly a couple of times. Finally, he gave a faint groan.

'Bethan, this is driving me a little crazy. It *is* crazy. We're trapped in this damned dangerous situation, and all I can think about is how much I'm enjoying holding you like this—all the other things that I want to be doing——'

'Is that such a bad thing?' she asked almost wistfully.

'Yes, it is! You're getting to be an obsession. And obsessions are dangerous things. They override everything else. They turn your life upside-down and hurl you into an emotional mess, so you don't know what you want any more.'

'I always thought you were the sort of man who knew exactly what he wanted,' Bethan said slowly.

'So did I,' Max agreed rather grimly. 'And until I met you, I had my life neatly mapped out.'

'Isn't that rather boring? Following a set path all the time, and never doing anything on impulse?'

'I'm thirty-seven years old. I don't need the highs and lows of an out-of-control love affair. I've outgrown that sort of thing.'

'Thirty-seven isn't exactly ancient. And it can be very nice to be out of control now and again—or so I've been told,' Bethan said slightly mischievously.

Despite the dark, despite the danger, she had begun to feel much less scared now. With a small sight of contentment, she snuggled a little closer to Max, deliberately ignoring his frustrated mutter. As long as she stayed where she was, she was sure she would be absolutely safe. For just a moment, a small voice inside her head warned her she wasn't being very wise. Without too much effort, though, she managed to ignore it. Surely there couldn't be anything wrong in being in the arms of the man she

loved? It certainly *felt* right. And, even if she knew
that love wasn't returned, maybe it wouldn't hurt to
pretend for a while that it was. Anyway, a lot of
people thought that being wanted was almost as
good as being loved.

Part of her knew perfectly well that she was in-
dulging in a dangerous delusion. Right now,
though, it just didn't seem to matter. Cut off from
the real world like this, all the old rules no longer
seemed to apply; she was free to make up new ones
as she went along.

Her face was pressed against the material of
Max's shirt. She sniffed appreciatively. The scent of
fresh, clean sweat was mixed with musky
undertones, where the material had been in contact
with Max's body. It was more stimulating than any
artificial perfume; it had an earthy quality which
made her senses tingle.

Max reached up and tried to disengage her arms
from his neck. 'Be a good girl, and let go of me. Just
for a few minutes,' he said coaxingly. 'I know you're
scared, but clinging to me like a limpet isn't going to
help matters. In fact, you could end up in an even
more dangerous situation,' he warned, in a voice
that had suddenly gone husky.

'I don't want to let go,' Bethan said dreamily.
'I'm perfectly happy right here.'

'Bethan, snap out of it!'

His terse order finally got through to her. She
lifted her head and stared at him, wishing she could
see him. In this pitch darkness, it was so hard to tell
what was really going through his head. In the past,
she had always had his eyes to guide her. Often, she
had found it unexpectedly easy to read the messages
emblazoned in their depths. Now, there was nothing

except her own instincts—and her deep need to stay near him.

With a small sigh, she buried her face back in the hollow of his shoulder. 'I think I'll just stay where I am, and chance the consequences.'

'Stop pushing your luck, Bethan,' Max told her a little grimly.

'If you really wanted to get rid of me, you could do it quite easily. You're a lot stronger than I am,' she pointed out. 'One hefty shove, and you'd be free of me.'

'And what if I don't want to give you that shove?'

'You just said that you did. You're contradicting yourself.'

'That's probably because I'm in a very contradictory mood,' came his sighed response. 'I want what I shouldn't have, and yet I *don't* want it because I'm afraid it'll turn my life inside out. I'm in a mess, Bethan,' he admitted throatily. 'And you're entirely responsible.'

His fingers had begun to travel restlessly down the line of her spine, as if he no longer had any control over them. They paused to explore the hollow in the small of her back, and then worked their way over the curve of her hips.

Max sighed again, but this time there was a shuddering quality to his breath as it was expelled from his lungs. Hearing it, Bethan lifted her own hand and let it rest against his face. Then she lightly traced the outline of his familiar features. Her fingertips moved gently over high cheekbones and the long, straight ridge of his nose. They fanned against his thick lashes, admired the strong line of his jaw, and then alighted, soft as a feather, on his lower lip. And there they lingered, issuing an unspoken invitation.

He moved his head a fraction, and his lips left a soft yet hot kiss in the palm of her hand. Then his warm breath brushed her face as he turned back to her, and she felt an answering touch against her own lower lip. It wasn't with his fingers, though, but with his tongue. With gentle softness, he lightly stroked and caressed, provoking a deep shiver of delight in her. The stroking became more insistent; an instant later, Max's tongue slid inside her mouth, and she shivered again with pleasure.

His kiss deepened and changed, becoming more demanding, forcing her to respond with equal fierceness. There was a new tautness in his muscles, and he shifted impatiently, so that she was wedged closer against him now.

'This is absolute insanity,' Max muttered against her ear.

But she hardly heard what he was saying. Most of her life, she seemed to have been looking for something she had never found. Love, she supposed. The one thing that had always been in such short supply, lost in the flood of material goodies and money that had always been such a very poor substitute. Well, perhaps this wasn't the real thing either; perhaps it was far too one-sided. It was the nearest she had ever got to it, though, and she wouldn't—*couldn't*—let go of it.

She wasn't naïve; she knew very well she might be unleashing a devil it would be impossible to tame. Still, though, she didn't hesitate. 'Don't stop,' she murmured unsteadily. 'Please, Max—don't stop.'

He held back for a few moments longer, as if something inside him was still stubbornly fighting it. Then his mouth swooped hungrily down on hers in a gesture of total defeat. In just seconds, his hands had swept away her cotton shirt. He abandoned her mouth and, before she had time to utter a moan of protest, he had buried his head in the swollen curves of her breasts. Heat curled up through her stomach as his breath burnt her skin and his hair brushed against her like softest swansdown. Then he moved again, lightly seizing the nearest stiffened peak, nibbling, then licking, and then finally covering it with loving kisses. Bethan closed her eyes at the fierce pleasure he was provoking in her, wanting more, and yet more.

'Like smooth silk,' Max murmured huskily, his words a little muffled by her delicate skin. 'My God, Bethan, you're beautiful!' Then he dragged in a deep breath that turned into a ragged sigh, 'I think I knew, right from the start, that you could so easily become an obsession,' he muttered. 'And now I'm letting it happen.'

Something inside Bethan stirred uneasily. Was an obsession the same thing as love? Then she pushed away that uncomfortable, unwelcome thought. Love, obsession—they were only words. What did it matter how he described what was happening between them? They were together, and that was the only thing of any real importance. And she was beginning to love him so completely and wholeheartedly that it would surely make up for any small uncertainties on his part.

Although she couldn't see him, she knew he was looking down at her now.

'I think I like you like this,' he murmured, and she was relieved to hear a much lighter note in his voice now, as if he had thrown off his introspective mood of only moments ago. His hand drifted down and gently caressed the flat plane of her stomach.

'Like what?'

'Submissive,' he told her, in a teasing tone. 'It's certainly a novelty!'

A little indignantly, she tried to struggle free of his exploring fingers. It was no use, though. With just one hand, he easily kept her exactly where he wanted her.

'Just because you're bigger and stronger, that doen't mean you can throw your weight around!' she said with mock sternness.

'But that's exactly what it *does* mean,' Max purred. 'It's the one advantage that us poor males have when we come up against the female of the species.' Then, despite the darkness, he homed in on her mouth with deadly accuracy, and very effectively silenced her for several minutes.

'Mmm,' he said thoughtfully, when he finally disengaged himself again. 'That was even nicer than I remember it from last time.'

Bethan, who was suddenly reduced to a melting heap, couldn't get out a single word.

He drew back a fraction. 'This *is* crazy,' he said in a resigned voice. 'You do know that, don't you?'

'Yes, I know,' she agreed in an unsteady voice. 'But Max——' She hesitated for a moment, then went on quietly, 'It does feel right.'

'I know,' he said a little roughly. 'But that doesn't always make it right. I keep thinking——'

'Don't think,' she broke in quickly, a faint note of panic entering her tone. 'Don't spoil things.'

Max sighed. 'I'm fast reaching the point where I'm willing to agree with just about everything you say.' His hand moved restlessly back to the curve of her breast and then rested there, his fingers curled round the warmth of her flesh, as if he found some comfort, some peace of mind, in the intimate contact. Then Bethan felt an abrupt change of mood sweep over him. His grip suddenly tightened and his thumb rhythmically rubbed the tip of her breast into a hard, aching response.

'I don't think I can fight this—not when I want it so much,' he muttered. She sensed his closeness as he loomed over her, then felt the weight of him, the aching hardness that was driving him on. Her eyes closed in anticipation of his kiss, his touch, his total sweet possession.

Before it came, though, a dull hammering sound echoed round the cavern. Max was the first to hear it. Bethan's own dazed and disordered senses weren't aware of anything until he raised his head, his entire body suddenly becoming tense.

'Max?' she said uncertainly. 'What—what is it?' Then she heard the sound which had distracted him. Immediately, she stiffened. 'Is it another cave-in?' she asked fearfully.

'No, sweetheart. Just someone saving us from our own folly,' he told her. The frustration was very clear in his voice, yet underneath she thought she could also hear a faint note of relief. 'I think we're about to be rescued.'

His words sent a massive wave of disappointment sweeping through her. She didn't *want* to be rescued. She knew it was perfectly ridiculous to feel like that, considering the danger they were in, but she just couldn't help it. She wanted to be trapped in this cave with Max for ever. This was the only place where she could feel truly sure of him. Once they were back in the real world again, everything could so easily go wrong, so many things could come between them . . .

But it was too late to think like that. Max was already moving away from her and beginning to fasten his shirt. With a small sigh, she fumbled around in the darkness for the buttons on her blouse. Of course she wanted to be rescued, she told herself severely. And there was no need to be so pessimistic; things didn't have to change once they were out of here. There was a new closeness between Max and herself now.

But he hasn't said he loves you, warned a small voice inside her head.

He didn't have to put it into words, she argued with herself defiantly. Some things were just understood between two people.

Then she sighed again, more heavily this time. She wasn't some little innocent. She knew that men were often motivated by a purely sexual drive. It was women who found it far more difficult to separate the emotional from the physical. Her unease and depression deepened, and her hands fumbled uncertainly as she finished fastening her blouse.

'If only a small section of the roof has come down, it shouldn't take them too long to reach us,' predicted Max.

'What? Oh—yes,' she muttered, only half taking in what he was saying. With an enormous effort, she tried to sound as practical as he was. 'Shouldn't we make our way to the tunnel, so we're close by when they break through?'

'We're safer here,' decided Max. 'There's always a chance they'll dislodge another chunk of roof while they're digging.'

They sat in silence after that, listening to the sounds of their rescuers as they very slowly drew nearer. Time seemed to take on an elastic quality, stretching on for ever. Bethan began to feel as if it were hours—even days—since she had been in Max's arms.

'Hello?' The loud, anxious voice echoed round the cavern, making her jump. Then a beam of light shone through from the tunnel, lifting the thick, oppressive darkness.

'Over here!' called Max.

A dark figure appeared behind the torch. 'It's me—Steve,' he announced. 'Are you both all right?'

That was rather a matter of opinion, Bethan thought, a little numbly. But Max was already assuring Steve they were both fine.

'Then we'd better get moving,' Steve told them. 'We've managed to clear a hole just about big enough to scramble through, but it looks pretty unstable. I don't think it would be a good idea to hang around.'

Max took hold of her hand and guided her out of the cavern, then along the tunnel. By the light of Steve's torch, they could make out an irregular hole, where a narrow passage had been cleared through the rubble.

'You go first,' Max said, pushing her forward. Then, as she looked at him a little anxiously, he added quickly, 'I'll be right behind you. You'll be quite safe.'

'What are you going to do?' she asked wryly. 'Hold the roof up single-handed if it starts to collapse?'

'Stop chattering and get moving!' He gave her a none-too-gentle shove. 'I want to get out of here.'

Obviously, Max didn't feel any sentimental attachment to this place, she told herself with a small pang. Then there wasn't time to brood about it any more because she had to concentrate on worming her way through the narrow, uneven passage their rescuers had cleared. It was dark, dusty and claustrophobic, and Bethan might have panicked if it hadn't been for her constant awareness of Max's presence only inches behind her.

Then she was finally crawling out the other end, tired, coughing, and glad of the arms that reached out to grip and steady her. Looking up, she saw Ahmed, and a couple of Egyptians she didn't recognise. Once they had made sure she was all right, they went back to help the other two men. When they were finally out, everyone rather hurriedly began to make their way back towards the cave entrance.

Bethan's feet were dragging now. Great waves of exhaustion had suddenly started to sweep over her, and she felt rather unpleasantly dizzy. It was reaction, she supposed. After all, it hadn't been an exactly uneventful day!

When they reached the entrance, Bethan was amazed to find that it was still daylight, the sun teetering on the horizon and filling the sky with fantastic streaks of vivid colour. She felt as if they had been trapped in that cavern for hours and hours.

She rubbed her eyes confusedly, and Max shot a sharp glance at her.

'Are you all right?'

'I'm beginning to feel completely wiped out,' she admitted.

'Just hang on for a while longer. We'll soon be back at camp.'

There was a faint pounding in her ears now, though, and she sat down rather abruptly, afraid she might fall over if she tried to keep standing. She was vaguely aware that someone was tying a rope under her arms, and a voice—Max's voice?—was gently assuring her everything was going to be fine.

Strong arms lowered her over the edge of the overhang, and then she was dangling in space. She might have been nervous if she had felt well enough to fully appreciate what was happening. After what seemed like a very long time, her feet touched the ground and there were more hands freeing her from the rope.

Blinking her rather blurred eyes, she looked up and saw Peter's familiar face hovering over her.

'Thank God you're all right,' he said with intense relief. 'I felt so damned helpless, stuck down here and not being able to do anything useful.'

'You organised the rescue, didn't you?' she said in a rather croaky and unsteady voice.

Peter nodded. 'I heard a rumble, so I knew there must have been some sort of cave-in. Because of my bloody stupid fear of heights, though, I couldn't get up to you, to find out if you were all right. I waited a while, praying you'd come out, but when nothing happened I knew you had to be trapped. I drove back to camp to radio for help, and found Steve was there. He'd got bored in Luxor, so he'd come back to work on some research notes. We decided it would be quicker if we tried to get you out ourselves, so we shot off to Ahmed's village, and rounded up Ahmed and a couple of his relatives. Then we came back here, and Steve and the other men went up to dig you out.'

Bethan somehow managed to get out a weak grin. 'Poor old Poppy! She's going to be furious when she gets back from Luxor and finds out she's missed all this drama.'

'It's the kind of excitement I could well do without,' Peter said rather grimly. 'I was terrified we wouldn't get you out, that——' He broke off and gave a small shudder. 'Let's not talk about it any more. At least, not right now. You're out and you're safe, and that's all that matters.'

Was it? Bethan wondered tiredly. Was that how Max felt as well? Had the rest of it been something that he would much prefer to forget?

As if thinking about him had somehow magically conjured up his presence, Max's voice cut into her confused and wandering thoughts.

'Can you make it to the Land Rover?'

'Yes, I think so.' There wasn't a lot of conviction in her voice, though, and he seemed to pick it up immediately. An instant later, he scooped her up, and Bethan didn't make a single murmur of protest. To hell with independence and Women's Lib! This was so comforting, so *nice*, being held against the hard warmth of a body that was now so familiar to her. She rubbed her cheek contentedly against the dusty material of Max's shirt, and curled her arms a little tighter around his neck.

'The night that we first met, you kept carrying me everywhere,' she reminded him.

'So I did. At the time, though, I didn't know it was going to become a habit,' he replied wryly.

'Some habits can be very pleasant.'

'I could certainly get used to this one,' came his unexpected and rather throaty admission.

He lowered her into the front seat of the Land Rover, and then slid in beside her. As he started up the engine, Bethan let her sleepy gaze rest on him, getting pleasure from just looking at him. Then she closed her eyes and half-dozed as the Land Rover bumped its way back to the camp.

When they arrived, Max took her straight to her tent and deposited her on the bed. Then he lit the small lamp, since it was almost dark now.

'This *is* like that first night,' she said, stifling a huge yawn. Then her eyes brightened mischievously. 'Only that time, you undressed me.'

'Mmm. Perhaps we'd better skip that part,' Max said, with marked reluctance. 'You're too tired, and I'm too——'

'You're too what?' she asked curiously, as he rather abruptly broke off.

'It doesn't matter.' There was a slightly harsh note in his voice now. 'I just don't think it would be a very good idea right now.'

Bethan gave a small shrug. She felt too drained to get involved in any conversation that was too deep or complicated. She snuggled further down into the bed, stretched her tired limbs, and then relaxed. She glanced up at Max again, and then couldn't help grinning. 'You look absolutely awful! You're covered in dirt and smudges, and that shirt's definitely never going to be the same, no matter how well it's laundered.'

Max grinned back at her. 'You're no pin-up yourself.' One finger idly flicked a dusty strand of her hair. 'I'm not sure that we've got enough water in camp to get you clean again.'

'Back in that cave, you told me I was beautiful,' she reminded him. Then she stiffened slightly. Had she reminded him of something that he preferred to forget?

But Max still seemed quite relaxed. 'The torch had gone out,' he reminded her. 'I was as blind as a bat at the time.'

'Next time I go fishing for compliments, I'll make sure you can see me,' she said lightly. 'That way, I'll know that you mean them.'

'I always mean what I say,' he replied in a steady voice. Then he glanced at his watch. 'It's getting late. I'd better leave you, so you can get some sleep.' He turned, but then paused for several seconds, as if he suddenly wanted to say something more. In the end, though, he gave a brusque shrug of his shoulders and rather quickly left the tent.

Bethan stared at the spot where he had been standing, for some reason wanting to hold on to the image of him for a few more minutes. As soon as he had gone, her throat had begun to feel oddly tight, and her eyes were rather hot and scratchy, almost as if she wanted to cry, but couldn't. That's ridiculous, she told herself irritably. You're tired, that's all. After a good night's sleep, everything will be fine; you'll be able to cope with things—no matter what happens.

Yet, although she was aching with tiredness, she couldn't get to sleep. Now and then, she heard the quiet murmur of voices outside the tent, but finally it went very quiet as the camp settled down for the night. She tossed restlessly. This was ridiculous! She was so exhausted, she *had* to fall asleep.

Then a waft of chill evening air drifted over her heated skin. Someone had just silently come into the tent.

She turned her head, and in the near-darkness could just make out the tall, dark figure now standing by the side of the bed.

'Max?' she said in an unsteady voice.

'Were you expecting someone else?'

His voice might have been teasing, but his tone certainly wasn't.

'Why have you come back?'

'Because I can't sleep,' he said roughly. 'And it looks as if you can't, either,' he added more huskily. 'Why not, Bethan?'

She swallowed hard. 'I don't know,' she whispered.

'Liar,' he said softly. Without another word, he pulled back the blanket and slid in beside her. 'Up in that cavern today, we started something that's got to be finished.' He said it as a simple statement of fact. He didn't give her a chance to protest, to deny it. Instead, he began to remove her clothes as if it were the most natural thing in the world.

Dazed and bewildered by what was happening, Bethan made no attempt to stop him. She didn't *want* to stop him. Not that she was sure she could have. Max was already moving on relentlessly, pushing her back on the bed, letting his mouth roam at will as he removed the last of her undies, delving into warm, intimate places and lingering there in obvious delight at what he found.

'Delicious,' he murmured. But there was a hot impatience in his voice now, as if he had been waiting a lifetime for this moment, and couldn't bear to wait one moment longer.

As he ripped off the last of his own clothes, Bethan instinctively moved to touch him. Strong muscles moved with supple power under her exploring fingers; she marvelled at the perfect proportions of his body, the breadth of his shoulders and the firm line of his spine. A grunt of frustration sounded in Max's throat as her explorations grew more bold. She realised he didn't intend to wait—couldn't wait. He had come here tonight out of sheer need. For perhaps the first time in his adult life, things were beyond his control. No subtlety, no expertise—only a wanting that had suddenly got completely out of hand, become too much to bear.

Propping himself on his arms, he slid over her. Although she had been expecting it, the first touch of his fiercely aroused body still came as a scalding shock. Sensing the deep quiver that ran through her, he somehow managed to keep very still for several seconds, giving her time to get used to it. His hands ran soothingly over her breasts, reassuring her, gentling her into an acceptance of what he so urgently wanted from her.

'Does it feel good?' he murmured thickly. 'It does for me. Tell me, Bethan!'

'Yes, it feels good,' she whispered shakenly.

Her heart was pounding as wildly and erratically as his own now. She seemed to be lost in a huge and still-swelling wave of love that was swallowing her up. Max gave a small groan, and his body beat its need against her with fresh, urgent persistence. Without hesitation, she opened herself up to him, gladly accepting the hard, sure body that immediately buried itself in her welcoming warmth.

There was no slow build-up, no gradual ascent to the climax of passion. Instead, the world instantly tipped over, spun round, and then seemed to somer-sault over and over. The resulting chaos was crazy and incredible, a torrent that swept away both of them, sending them whirling out of control down a deep, dark path that ended in a maelstrom of exquisite delight.

Bethan had no breath left for anything, not even his name. Instead, she held on to him very tightly, until the world finally became still again. And even then, she couldn't let go. Max didn't seem to mind. His arms hugged her close, and his harsh breathing fanned the side of her neck, gradually slowing until it was only a little faster than normal.

Even then, neither of them spoke. Max finally eased himself on to his side, so that he was no longer crushing her. Bethan instantly curled up against him again, wanting the warm physical contact between them to go on for ever. Lethargic and light-headed, she seemed to float in his arms, while her mind dazedly drifted back over what had happened. Had that sweat-soaked and wanton woman really been her? She hadn't known she was capable of such a headlong tumble into raw desire. And Max's own brooding sensuality had been even fiercer than her own, yet it hadn't scared her. From the moment when he had first touched her, all she had wanted was to share in it, gloriously and completely. She gave a small shake of her head. Love certainly did incredible things to people!

Then the sleep that had eluded her earlier finally began to sweep over her, irresistible this time. Her heavy eyes drooped shut, she gave one last murmur of contentment, and then slid gently into a deep, relaxed sleep.

CHAPTER NINE

WHEN Bethan finally woke up again next morning, she was alone. For a couple of minutes, she lay there dazedly wondering if last night had been a delicious, erotic dream. Perhaps she had been delirious with tiredness, and imagined the entire thing.

Then she shook her head. Her imagination wasn't *that* vivid—or inventive! But if it really had happened—where did they go from here?

She decided that, for now, she didn't want to worry about it. Things would work themselves out, she was sure of it. Humming softly under her breath, she swung herself off the camp bed and then glanced at her reflection in the small mirror on the table. A second later, she groaned. It certainly wasn't a raving beauty that was looking back at her. Her skin was streaked with grime, her hair was clogged with dust, and there were still dark shadows of tiredness under her eyes.

She definitely had to do something about her appearance before she saw Max again. Cautiously, she peered out through the tent flap. The camp seemed to be deserted. She gave a quick frown. Where was everyone? Where was Max? Then she glanced down and saw two buckets of water standing just outside the tent. That instantly cheered her up. Two whole buckets—sheer luxury! That was more than double their usual daily ration that was allowed for washing. Since every drop of water had to be laboriously brought to the camp in large containers, it was always very strictly rationed.

She dragged the buckets into the tent, stripped off, and then scrubbed herself clean from head to toe. There was even enough water to wash the worst of the dust from her hair. When she had finally finished, she took a more confident look in the mirror, and then gave a satisfied smile. She still wouldn't win any prizes, but her hair would soon dry to its usual glossy shine, and her eyes . . . She looked again at her eyes. She had never seen them look like that before, so sparkling, so totally alive.

Now came the hard part, though. She had to find Max, look into *his* eyes, and see if last night had meant the same to him as it had to her. Feeling suddenly very nervous, and with an odd sinking sensation deep in her stomach, she stepped outside the tent. The heat of the sun immediately hit her with its usual force but for once she didn't notice it. Instead, her gaze anxiously skimmed round the camp site. It still seemed totally deserted, though. Where had Max gone?

She made some coffee, then sat outside to drink it so that the sun would dry her still damp hair. The hot, sweet drink didn't help to settle her nerves, though. Instead, she could feel the anxiety building up inside her. Why wasn't Max here? Was this his way of telling her that last night had been a one-off? That it had been good at the time, but he didn't intend to repeat it? She began to feel a little sick. Please God, no, she prayed a little frantically. She didn't think she could cope with that.

Then she lifted her head and saw the familiar sight of Max's Land Rover approaching the camp. Her pulses immediately flipped into overdrive, and her head felt oddly woozy. Calm down! she ordered herself shakily. It's only Max.

But just saying his name to herself triggered off a fresh surge of nervous shivers. She realised she was actually scared of seeing him, terrified of looking into his amber eyes and seeing only a cool friendliness instead of a hot flare of response. She couldn't remember ever feeling so unsure of herself, so apprehensive about the future. For a couple of seconds, she almost hated him for making her feel like a jittery schoolgirl.

Then the door of the Land Rover opened, and Bethan's eyebrows flew up in surprise. It wasn't Max who had got out, but an expensively dressed blonde. Bethan's gaze flew over the white cotton safari suit and the perfectly matching accessories. Not very practical, she decided. But she had the impression that this woman was dressing for effect; she probably had several other equally stunning outfits she could change into if she got a speck of dirt on this one.

The woman immediately began to walk towards Bethan. It was almost as if she had come out here with the express intention of seeing her. Bethan looked at her curiously as she drew nearer, and then suddenly something clicked inside her head. A cool, beautiful blonde—and Bethan had the sickening feeling that she could put a name to her. Caroline—Max's fiancée.

Briefly, she closed her eyes. She didn't feel up to a confrontation, not this morning. Then she opened them again, to find the blonde woman standing just a couple of feet away.

She studied Bethan with frank curiosity. 'So, you're Bethan Lawrence,' she said at last in a slow drawl. 'You're not quite what I expected—much more exotic. Almost like a gypsy, in fact, with all that black hair and dark eyes. I didn't know Max had a taste for that sort of thing.' She managed to make it sound like a total insult, and Bethan instantly bristled. Before she could say anything, though, the woman went on, 'I suppose I should introduce myself. I'm Caroline Leslie. I dare say Max has spoken of me.'

'He's mentioned you once or twice,' said Bethan in a cold voice. 'I believe you're an old friend.' Her slight but obvious emphasis on the word 'old' brought a frosty glint to Caroline's eyes. Then she relaxed again, and her perfect mouth curved into a faint smile.

'Well, since you know who I am, you know why I'm here,' she said calmly. 'I've been hearing one or two disturbing rumours lately, so I thought it was time I flew out and sorted out the situation.' Her gaze flicked over Bethan. 'I don't know what you and Max have been up to the last couple of weeks—and to be frank, I don't really care—but whatever it was, I want you to know that it's over now. Max is mine,' she went on, her tone suddenly hard. 'And that's the way I intend it to stay. And if you've got any doubts about it, I'll tell you one more thing. Max and I are flying back to England later today—together.'

'Doesn't Max have any say in the matter?' Bethan somehow managed to get out.

'Max wants the same things that I do,' Caroline replied, her tone totally confident. 'That's why we get on so well together, and why we'll have a very successful marriage.'

The other woman's attitude was so patronising that Bethan felt a strong desire to kick her elegant shins.

'If you and Max get on so well together, how come he's spent so much time away from you?' she got out through gritted teeth.

Caroline raised one eyebrow, looking almost bored now. 'You want the truth? I made the mistake of not going to bed with him. I thought it would make him more eager,' she said in a detached voice. 'Instead, he's got himself involved with someone totally unsuitable—you.'

'I got the impression that you didn't *want* to go to bed with him,' Bethan said bluntly.

The other woman's eyes narrowed. 'You've obviously been having some very interesting conversations. But since everyone's being so frank, let's get a few facts straight. I'll do whatever's got to be done to make sure that Max wants to stay with me.' Her voice was suddenly edged with pure steel. 'You think I don't know how to keep Max satisfied? Wrong, little girl! I might not like sex, I might think it's very over-rated and slightly absurd, but I can put on a damned good performance when it's necessary. And if it's not enough for Max, if he's the sort of man who's always going to need to get some extra excitement elsewhere, then I can easily learn to live with that.'

Bethan stared at her in pure horror. 'That's not marriage,' she said in a near-whisper. 'That's purgatory!'

Caroline shrugged. 'I'm not some silly little romantic. I know exactly what I want from marriage—and Max is the man who can give it to me.'

'You mean money,' Bethan accused.

'Yes,' she said coolly. 'And the sort of social life that someone in Max's position can give me. I don't intend to give that up for anyone—and certainly not for a little nobody like you.'

'Perhaps Max ought to decide that,' said Bethan tautly.

'What are you going to do?' asked Caroline, shooting a challenging look at her. 'Go running to him and demand that he chooses between us? That might not be a very good idea,' she warned, a hint of triumph lightening her beautiful but cold eyes. 'Max and I had a long talk this morning. We got a lot of things straightened out. And of course, once Max told me who you were, I began to understand why he got himself involved with you.'

'What do you mean—who I am?' demanded Bethan.

'Why—that you're Howard Lawrence's daughter.'

Bethan was briefly stunned. 'Max told you about that?'

'Of course he did.' Caroline shot her a pitying look. 'You still won't accept it, will you? Max and I *understand* each other. I know exactly how his mind works, how he got himself into this ridiculous situation. It was inevitable that he wouldn't just walk away from you, not once he found out who you were. Believe it or not, Max has got a very active conscience. He felt extremely guilty when he realised you'd been left penniless because of the way he handled your father's estate. More than that, he began to feel a sense of responsibility towards you. Unfortunately,' Caroline added in a condescending tone that totally grated on Bethan's already raw nerves, 'you started to confuse that sense of responsibility with a very different emotion. Embarrassing for Max, of course—and it was very naughty of him to take advantage of it—but men are like that, aren't they? No sense of right and wrong—at least, not where sex is concerned.'

'Perhaps *you're* the one who's confused,' Bethan got out in a choked voice.

'Oh, no, I don't think so,' replied Caroline with absolute certainty. 'So perhaps it's time you started to face up to facts. Max doesn't love you. In fact, I don't think he's capable of truly loving anyone. That's why he's picking his marriage partner with his head, and

not his heart. And it's why our marriage will be a
complete success. We won't make any impossible
demands on each other—it will be a very civilised, very
pleasant arrangement between two mature people who
know exactly what they want.' She gave Bethan one
last superior smile. 'You still don't believe me? Then
let me tell you where Max is right now. He's in Luxor,
booking us both a flight back to England. And once
we're home, I'll make very sure that he won't want to
leave ever again.'

With a dismissive gesture of her elegant head, she
turned and strolled off, leaving Bethan feeling
completely shattered. She had thought she was
beginning to know Max. Yet the man Caroline had
been speaking about was a total stranger, someone
whose mind operated on such a different wavelength
that there was no chance she would ever be able to
understand him. Which of them was right? she
wondered a little desperately. Did she or Caroline
know the real Max Lansdelle?

If Max was really in Luxor, booking plane tickets
for himself and Caroline, then the answer was pretty
obvious. Bethan tiredly shook her aching head. She
hadn't known it was possible to feel this confused and
miserable.

She was half-dreading Max's return, although she
desperately wanted to see him again. A small surge of
resentment spread through her at the way he was mes-
sing up all her emotions. All her life, she had had an
inner confidence that had carried her through count-
less difficult situations. Even her father's death had
only knocked her off balance for a short time; then she
had hauled herself to her feet again, determined to
battle on. But Caroline's revelations had really left her
floundering. She felt as if someone had whipped the

ground right out from under her, and then forgotten to
put it back again.

It was late morning before Peter's jeep came roaring
back into camp. Caroline had disappeared by this
time, taking herself off into one of the tents. Probably
didn't want to let the sun get to that pale, flawless skin
of hers, Bethan thought with uncharacteristic
bitchiness.

Peter and Max got out the jeep, then the two men
stood talking quietly for a couple of minutes. Finally,
Bob turned and walked off, and Max began to walk
purposefully in Bethan's direction.

Bethan swallowed hard, wishing her throat didn't
feel so uncomfortably dry and tight. For a few seconds,
she felt an awful urge to make a bolt for it. Instead,
though, she stayed exactly where she was, every one of
her nerves raw and quivering.

Coming to a halt in front of her, Max looked down
at her with his familiar, fierce amber gaze. Then he
slid into the seat which Caroline had sat in earlier.

'How do you feel?' he asked without preamble.
'Any ill-effects from yesterday?'

Yes! she wanted to shout at him. I fell in love with
you, damn you!

Instead, though, she sat there with a rather fixed,
polite smile on her face.

'A bit of a headache, that's all. Apart from that, I'm
fine.'

Max frowned. 'I suppose you're going to have to
know sooner or later. Caroline's turned up.'

'I already know. We've—we've met.'

His frown deepened. 'I told her to stay away from
you,' he growled. Then he looked straight at her, his
gaze glowing more hotly. 'I looked in on you this
morning, but you were still asleep. I wanted to wake

you, but——'

'But you thought it might not be a good idea, with Caroline hovering in the background?' Bethan finished for him, slightly sarcastically.

'No! That was definitely not what I meant. Damn it, what's she been saying to you?' he demanded.

'Nothing of any importance,' she said stiffly. 'But you must have told *her* quite a lot. About my father, for instance.'

'There were a lot of things I had explain to her,' he said, a trace of anger creeping into his voice. 'I thought I owed her that, at least. Look, Bethan, I know this is a hell of a mess. I never expected Caroline to turn up like this——'

'No, I bet you didn't,' she cut in, her tone as sharp as his own. 'But it's all right, Max, I'm not going to make an embarrassing scene. I just want to know one thing.'

'What?'

'Are you going back to England?' she asked him directly. Then she virtually stopped breathing as she waited for his answer.

It seemed to take for ever for him to reply. At last, though, he gave a brief nod of his head. 'Yes, I am. I've got a flight booked for late this afternoon.'

'This afternoon?' Hard though she tried, she couldn't keep the utter dismay out of her voice. Her features became even more rigid. 'And I suppose Caroline's flying back with you?'

'Stop trying to twist things,' Max said tersely. Then he ran his fingers irritably through his hair. 'Look, I'm in a foul mood, so don't push me. Just about everything's gone wrong today. And I wanted things to be very different——'

'All I want is a simple answer to my question,'

Bethan interrupted him evenly. 'Is Caroline going with you?'

'Yes, damn it! She is. But I'm not flying back because of her. I phoned my office while I was in Luxor, and it turns out they're in the middle of a major crisis. They've been trying to contact me for the past couple of days. I've got to get back and sort it out before the whole thing blows up in our face. Huge sums of money are involved——'

'And it's just a coincidence that Caroline's flying back on the same plane?'

'Will you stop glaring at me with that accusing look on your face?' Max said fiercely. 'Caroline's flying back with me because I want to talk to her. I think she deserves a couple of hours of my time.' His gaze fixed on her darkly. 'What do you want me to do? Book you on the same flight? Use your head, Bethan! Can you imagine what it would be like, with all three of us on the same plane?'

'At least it wouldn't be boring.' Her poor attempt at a joke fell totally flat. She lifted her head and looked at Max a little defiantly. 'What am I supposed to do, then? Sit here and wait for you?'

'That's precisely what I want you to do,' he told her in a rather calmer tone.

Bethan blinked. 'You do?'

'I'll be back in a couple of days. That should give me enough time to get everything sorted out.'

'But Caroline said——'

Max's face darkened again. 'Who are you going to believe? Caroline or me?' And when she still hesitated, he gripped hold of her arm and gave it an impatient shake. 'Which one of us, Bethan?'

'You,' she got out in a rather strangled whisper.

A look of satisfaction settled over his face. He raised

her hand to his mouth, and let his lips burn a quick, hungry kiss on to her open palm.

'There's a great deal I want to say to you,' he said a little huskily. 'But there's no time for anything right now. Not even a decent goodbye kiss. I've got a hundred things to do before my flight leaves, and I've got to get moving straight away. There'll be plenty of time when I get back, though. Just make sure that you're here, waiting for me.'

Reluctantly, he tore his hand away from hers. He shot her one last hotly intimate smile that made her nerves melt, then he rapidly walked away, as if he had to leave immediately or he wouldn't be able to tear himself away from her at all.

All too soon, he left the camp, and Caroline went with him. Slowly, Bethan emerged from the daze in which she had been drifting. Was she crazy to trust him? Probably, she told herself with a sigh, but what else could she do? She loved him, so she just had to sit here and wait for him, as he had instructed.

And what about Caroline? She pushed that question to the very back of her mind. She didn't want to think about Caroline. That way, she could pretend that she didn't even exist.

The small camp somehow seemed very empty once Max had gone. The appropriate officials had been notified of the treasure she and Max had discovered, but Bethan found she couldn't get very excited about it. She wasn't even particularly interested in seeing it again. Anyway, it would be some time before any of the precious gold objects were brought out of the cavern. Before anything could be moved, the tunnel leading to the cavern had to be completely cleared and the roof expertly shored up, so there was no chance of another cave-in.

Peter decided he would continue with his original excavation while they were waiting for the authorities to sanction work on the cavern.

'It would be marvellous if I could find that tomb, on top of you and Max discovering all that treasure,' he told Bethan enthusiastically. 'And I'm sure I'm near to it. Just a few more days, and I think I might start uncovering something important.'

Privately, though, Bethan was beginning to think that Bob was never going to find this tomb with which he was so obsessed. She didn't say that to his face, though. It was his dream, the one thing that gave his life purpose. And she was beginning to understand about dreams. For the first time in her life, she had one of her own.

'Every time I look at you, you've got a rather silly grin on your face,' complained Poppy, a few days later. 'And you hardly ever hear me when I talk to you. Really, Bethan, I thought you were a sensible girl!'

'I am sensible,' Bethan said, a little indignantly.

'Well, I don't think it was very bright to fall for Max Lansdelle,' Poppy said bluntly.

'How can you say that, when you don't even know him very well?'

'I know that he isn't here,' retorted Poppy.

'He's coming back.'

'Is he?' Her tone became softer. 'Look, Bethan, I'm not trying to upset you, but you are behaving like a bit of an innocent. Don't you know that men will say *anything* to get out of an awkward situation? What's the best way to sidle off without any shouting matches, floods of tears, and insults being hurled around all over the place? Tell the girl you're coming back, of course,' she finished. 'Provided she believes you, you can scoot off without a backward glance. With luck, you'll even get a farewell kiss to send on your way.'

'Max *is* coming back,' Bethan insisted stubbornly. She had to believe that. She *had* to.

'How long did he say he'd be away?'

'He—he didn't say. Not exactly,' Bethan lied.

'It's been four days since he left,' Poppy reminded her.

'I know that! Sorry,' she muttered. 'I didn't mean to snap.'

'I know you didn't,' Poppy said sympathetically. 'And for all I know, he could be on his way back now. But I saw Caroline, remember? She was a bitch—but a gorgeous bitch. I wouldn't like to be up against that sort of competition.'

Bethan knew that Poppy's words weren't meant unkindly. It didn't help, though, to hear all her private anxieties and fears put into words. It was so easy to imagine what might have happened. Once back with Caroline again, Max might begin to realise what a very suitable wife she would make—and how *unsuitable* Bethan was, with her flamboyant looks and outspoken tongue. And if that wasn't the case, why wasn't he here? He had already been away twice as long as he had said he would be. How much longer was she going to have to wait?

For as long as it takes, she told herself stubbornly. It would be worth waiting a whole lifetime for a man like Max.

But the four days lengthened into five, then six. By the time a whole week had gone by, Bethan's stomach seemed to be permanently knotted into a painful ache. Poppy was tactful enough not to say another word on the subject, but it was very obvious what she was thinking. Nor could Bethan blame her. It was pretty clear by then that Max wasn't coming back; probably, he had never had any intention of coming back.

Depressed and disillusioned, Bethan slid further and further into a mood of apathetic misery, until Poppy finally lost her patience. Coming into the tent late one morning and finding Bethan still sitting on the camp bed, staring blankly into space, Poppy gave her a small shake.

'Look, you can't spend the rest of your life sitting around looking love-sick! All you're doing is getting on everyone's nerves.'

'Thanks for the sympathy,' Bethan retorted, briefly jolted out of her apathy.

'You don't want sympathy—just someone to give you a good kick, to try and get you back to normal again,' Poppy said bluntly.

Bethan wrinkled her nose. 'Have I been that much of a pain?'

'Yes,' Poppy said uncompromisingly. 'But I suppose everyone's like that when love turns round and kicks them in the teeth. Whenever it happens to me, I take to my bed for a week, don't eat and cry buckets. I always feel much better afterwards,' she said, with a grin.

'I don't think that would work in my case,' Bethan said gloomily. 'Have you got any other suggestions?'

'Go back to England,' Poppy said promptly. And, when Bethan looked a little surprised, she went on, 'It's the only thing that makes sense. There's no point in hanging around here, all mopey and broody. Anyway, this place only reminds you of Max. It would be much better to go back home, and get back to work.'

'There's not much waiting for me in England,' confessed Bethan. 'A bedsitter, and a job that I don't

even like. And I'm not even sure they'll take me back,'
she added dolefully. 'My holiday leave was up days
ago. I should be back at my desk.'

'A small white lie won't hurt,' advised Poppy. 'Tell
them you got laid low with a bug while you were in Egypt.'

Bethan grimaced. 'That's not so very far from the
truth. I *did* meet up with a bug—his name was Roger!
He's the reason I ended up here. If the little creep
hadn't jumped on me while we were touring the
tombs, I wouldn't have dashed off and got stuck up a
cliff—I wouldn't have met Max——' She sighed.
'Funny how things work out, isn't it?'

'Hilarious!' said Poppy drily. 'So, what are you
going to do? Mope around here for a few more days?
Or go home?'

Bethan's shoulders slumped in a gesture of defeat.

'I suppose I haven't got much choice. I'd better go
home.'

The sun was shining in England, but it seemed a
weak, insipid brightness after the hot blaze she had
grown used to in Egypt.

Going back to work wasn't quite the ordeal she had
thought it would be. They accepted without question
her excuse of having caught a bug in Egypt which had
delayed her return. Bethan felt rather guilty about
having to lie to them, but she needed to keep this job,
at least until she could find something better.
Financially, she just couldn't afford to be out of work.
And on top of that, she suspected she would go
downhill fast if she had nothing to do except sit at
home all day, brooding over Max.

To her relief, apart from a few polite enquiries, no
one asked too many questions about her holiday. And
Roger rather pointedly ignored her, for which she was

thoroughly grateful.

It required a huge effort to carry on as if everything were normal. To talk to people; smile at them; eat, drink and sleep; keep behaving as if the business of living wasn't the flat, pointless exercise that she knew it to be.

By the end of the week, she was beginning to feel as if she were losing the battle. She felt an awful temptation to stand up in the middle of that beautifully designed and bustling office, and just yell out that she couldn't cope with any of it any more. She was hurting inside, and no one seemed to *care;* no one was really looking at her and seeing what a mess she was in, and she felt as if she were physically and mentally falling apart.

That afternoon, the agency was particularly busy. Bethan dealt automatically with a non-stop stream of enquiries and visiting clients. When one more dark, immaculate business suit presented itself in front of her, she didn't even look up.

'Can I help you?' she said in a flat tone.

'Yes, you damned well can!' snarled a familiar voice. Her head shot up and she found herself gazing straight into a pair of blazing amber eyes. 'You can tell me why the hell you didn't wait for me in Egypt,' went on Max in the same furious tone.

Bethan simply gaped at him.

He reached over the desk and gave her a none-too-gentle shake.

'I'm not leaving until you give me an answer,' he warned grimly.

Everywhere in the office, heads were swivelling round and gazes fixing on them with open curiosity. Bethan felt the blood beginning to rush into her face.

'I—I did wait for you,' she muttered. Then, more

indignantly, 'But you didn't come!'

'Of course not. But I explained why in the telegram I sent you. Was it too much of a hardship to hang on for just a few more days?' Max demanded harshly.

Bethan shook her head in confusion. 'I didn't get any telegram. I waited for over a week, then I thought—I thought——'

'That I'd run out on you?' said Max incredulously. 'Do you really think I'd do something like that?' He gripped hold of her arm and levered her to her feet.

'What are you doing?' she squeaked.

'We're getting out of here. We need to talk, and we can't do it here, with half the office listening in.'

'I can't just leave,' she objected. 'You'll have to wait until I've finished work.'

'I'm not waiting another minute,' Max growled. And, to her acute embarrassment—and everyone else's amusement—he marched her out of the office.

A few minutes later, she found herself sitting beside him in his car as he headed out of London. She opened her mouth to say something, but then rather helplessly shut it again. The events of the afternoon seemed to have left her virtually dumbstruck.

Max drove very fast, but very competently. Soon, they had left the outskirts of London behind and were heading into Kent. Max turned off the main road and threaded the car expertly through a series of narrow minor roads. They swept through a small village set between the wooded folds of two low hills, and out the other side; then they suddenly swung into a wide drive, coming to a halt outside a red-brick house that nestled comfortably in a tree and flower-studded garden.

Bethan stared round. 'Is this where you live?'

'Why are you looking so surprised?'

'I just thought——'

'Thought what?' queried Max. 'That I'd live in some functional flat in the centre of town?'

'Yes, I suppose so,' she admitted.

'I did for a while, but I didn't like it. I wanted a home, somewhere I could relax and be at peace. This seemed like a good place.'

'It's beautiful,' Bethan said quietly, and her verdict seemed to please him.

He got out of the car and opened the door for her. 'Come inside. See if you like that as well.'

She followed him into the house, and her face lit up with pleasure as she saw the interior. It was furnished in an unexpectedly old-fashioned style, with the emphasis on comfort rather than elegance. There were chairs with soft, fat cushions, solid tables in a dark, rich wood, thick rugs casually scattered over polished wooden floors, and landscape paintings which glowed with warm colour.

Max led her to a drawing-room at the back of the house. French windows opened on to a terrace that overlooked the secluded garden. He opened them to let in warm, fresh air and the scent of flowers; then he turned back to her.

'Still like it?'

'I love it. But there are a lot of things I just don't understand.'

His gaze fixed on her piercingly. 'Such as what?'

'Well—why you've brought me here, for a start. I don't even know how you *found* me,' she confessed. 'I nearly died of shock when I looked up and saw you standing there!'

'Good,' said Max grimly. 'Because you've certainly given me a couple of shocks over the past few days. The first one was going back to the camp and finding you'd gone. And the second one hit me when I realised I didn't have the slightest idea *where* you'd gone. Poppy told me you were going back to your old address and job, but where the hell were they? I certainly didn't know, and nor did anyone else.'

'I meant to leave my address with Poppy, but I forgot,' mumbled Bethan.

Max glared at her. 'Which put me through a couple of days of sheer hell. I couldn't think of any damned way to find you! Then, when I was just about ready to explode with frustration, I suddenly remembered you'd once told me that you worked at an advertising agency. It was a pretty slim lead, but it was the only one I had, so I got on to it straight away.' He gave a snort of disgust. 'I must have tried every agency in London before I finally hit the right one.'

She looked at him a little uncertainly. 'Am I really worth all that effort?'

His dark brows drew together in a glowering frown. 'I've no idea. But I suppose we've got the rest of our lives to find out.'

Her eyes flew wide open. 'Is that—well, is that a—a proposal?' she somehow got out in a disbelieving stutter.

'I suppose it is,' he growled.

'Mmm,' she said, slightly disapprovingly. 'It wasn't put very graciously.'

'That's probably because I don't feel very gracious at the moment,' Max muttered in the same surly tone. 'I'm not much good at this sort of thing.'

'You're certainly not,' she agreed, more cheerfully. 'Are you absolutely sure you're proposing to the right person? Caroline would be a much suitable wife for you, you know.'

'I know that,' he said rather impatiently. 'But I

don't want her. I want you.'

Her face briefly became shadowed. 'I thought you'd gone back to her,' she confessed. 'That once you'd got back to England, you'd realised it was her you wanted, not me.'

'Idiot!' he said, a little roughly. then in a calmer voice, he went on, 'I told you, Caroline and I were never officially engaged. I knew she would be an ideal wife—at least, as far as my career was concerned. She had the right connections, she knew how to be the perfect hostess, and there was the added advantage that she was stunning to look at. There was always a hint of coldness under all that beauty, though. I never seemed to be able to get through to her, to arouse any strong emotions in her. For a while, I thought it wouldn't matter, that it would be relaxing to have a marriage where there were no great passions or violent disagreements. Then I met you, and I had to rearrange all my ideas. You came crashing into my life and knocked it right off course. Suddenly, I started wanting very different things—things which I knew I could never get from Caroline.'

'Then why did you fly back to England with her?' asked Bethan in a small voice.

'When I found out she had turned up at the camp, I was furious,' said Max, pacing up and down now a little restlessly. 'No man likes to have the two women in his life turn up at the same time!' Then his mouth relaxed into a faint grin. 'If you remember, I was in a pretty filthy temper that day.'

'Yes, you were,' Bethan agreed fervently.

'I'm sorry if I practically bit your head off. You'll have to learn to cope with my black moods. Fortunately, I don't get them very often. Anyway, I was angry because I'd already had a long talk with

Caroline that morning, and tried to explain how things were. She still went to the camp, though, and tried to make trouble for you.'

'So when she tried to convince me everything was fine between you, she was just bluffing,' Bethan said slowly.

'She certainly was,' Max agreed a trifle grimly.

'How did she know about us?'

'Apparently, Peter let something slip during one of his phone calls back home. That piece of gossip was passed along the grapevine until it finally reached Caroline. She came racing out to Egypt, determined to get me back again. Unfortunately, she didn't know that it was already too late by then. That it was already over between us—at least, as far as I was concerned. She refused to accept it, though, so in the end I decided it would be best to book her on the same flight I was taking back home. That would give me several hours to talk to her and convince her it really was finished between us. And to apologise for breaking it off rather brutally. I felt I owed her that.' Max gave a grimace. 'Caroline never gives up, though. I found that out on our first night back in England. She came to my hotel room in the middle of the night, stripped down to the sexiest undies I've ever seen, and did her best to seduce me!'

'Poor Max,' murmured Bethan with mock sympathy. 'You have been through a very trying time.'

'Believe it or not, it was a total turn-off. And I told her so—rather bluntly,' he said ruefully.

Bethan remembered how Caroline had spoken about Max, seeming to see him as little more than a meal-ticket, and she couldn't dredge up more than a very small pang of sympathy for the other woman.

'Well, since you've well and truly ditched Caroline,

that means you're stuck with me,' she said, with a pleased smile. 'I know I'm probably not the perfect wife for a merchant banker, but pop me into the hairdresser's for a couple of hours and then stick me into a decent dress, and you'd be surprised how respectable I can look. And I'm fairly good at the social graces. If you want me to help entertain important clients, I won't embarrass you. It'll be boring, but I can do it.'

'I don't want you to act as some kind of unpaid hostess,' Max said fiercely. 'I want you to talk to, argue with—make love to,' he finished, his amber eyes beginning to glow hotly.

Bethan swallowed hard. 'I think that's what I want, too.'

'Then you're saying yes?' His voice sounded unexpectedly tense.

'Of course,' she said immediately. 'Yes, yes, *yes*! I love you, you idiot. What else did you think I'd say?'

He was holding her hands very tightly by now. 'I thought you might not want to be tied down just yet,' he admitted huskily. 'When we talked in Egypt, you didn't seem to know what you wanted to do with the rest of your life. I thought that marriage might not figure in your plans for the future. That there might be more interesting things that you wanted to try first.'

'I can't think of anything that would be more interesting than marriage to you!' She grinned. 'Remember I said that I'd never found anything yet I was good at? Well, I think I'm going to be good at this. And at having kids, too—as long as they're yours. Oh, there might be a lot of other things I'll want to do, later on,' she added. 'I don't even know what they are yet, but there's no rush. I've got the rest of my life to find out what they are. Right now, *you're* all that I want.'

Max visibly relaxed. 'This weekend, I'll take you

home to meet my parents,' he told her. 'They might get a bit upset if they don't get to meet my prospective bride before the wedding—which will be very soon,' he promised throatily.

Bethan gazed at him anxiously. 'Will they like me? Approve of me?'

'They might not approve of you,' Max said cheerfully, 'but they'll certainly like you. And once you've given them their first grandchild, they'll absolutely adore you.'

Bethan sighed with relief. 'That's good. I want to be part of your family, Max. I don't have any left of my own.'

His grip on her hands tightened. 'You'll always have me. I love you, sweetheart, and I'm always going to be here.'

As if to emphasise his words, his mouth closed over hers with fierce intent, savouring the touch and taste of her. With a small groan of delight, Bethan melted against him. His kiss was tantalisingly brief, though—a hungry swoop that left her aching for more.

With obvious frustration, he pushed her away from him, and then held her at a distance.

'I promised myself that I wouldn't lay a finger on you until after we were married,' he told her.

Bethan's mouth curled into a slow smile. 'Such willpower,' she purred. 'So very commendable!' She slid one finger between the buttons of his shirt, and tickled his chest. 'Do you think you'll be able to keep that promise?' she murmured.

'I will if you don't keep teasing me half to death,' Max said a little thickly. 'And if I can have a brief kiss now and then, to stop me going completely out of my head.'

Bethan looked up at him. 'And when do you think

you'll be needing the next kiss?' she asked demurely.

He gave a small groan. 'Right now!'

It was longer and greedier than the last one, and when it was over she could feel his pulses beating as wildly as her own.

'This isn't going to work,' he said in a half-strangled voice. 'It's been the same ever since I met you, Bethan. All or nothing.'

She gazed lovingly into the familiar amber glow of his eyes. 'Which do you want it to be, Max?'

'All,' he said simply.

And, with a sigh of pure happiness, she moved into the strong, possessive circle of his arms.

Harlequin Presents®

Coming Next Month

Available in August wherever paperback books are sold, or through
Harlequin Reader Service:

In the U.S.
901 Fuhrmann Blvd.
P.O. Box 1397
Buffalo, N.Y. 14240-1397

In Canada
P.O. Box 603
Fort Erie, Ontario
L2A 5X3

You'll flip . . . your pages won't!
Read paperbacks *hands-free* with

Book Mate • I

The perfect "mate" for all your romance paperbacks

Traveling • Vacationing • At Work • In Bed • Studying • Cooking • Eating

Perfect size for all standard paperbacks, this wonderful invention makes reading a pure pleasure! Ingenious design holds paperback books OPEN and FLAT so even wind can't ruffle pages — leaves your hands free to do other things. Reinforced, wipe-clean vinyl-covered holder flexes to let you turn pages without undoing the strap . . . supports paperbacks so well, they have the strength of hardcovers!

Pages turn WITHOUT opening the strap

SEE-THROUGH STRAP

Reinforced back stays flat

Built in bookmark

BOOK MARK

BACK COVER HOLDING STRIP

10 x 7¼ . opened
Snaps closed for easy carrying, too

Available now. Send your name, address, and zip code, along with a check or money order for just $5.95 + .75¢ for postage & handling (for a total of $6.70) payable to Reader Service to:

Reader Service
Bookmate Offer
901 Fuhrmann Blvd.
P.O. Box 1396
Buffalo, N.Y. 14269-1396

Offer not available in Canada
* New York and Iowa residents add appropriate sales tax.

BM-G

Harlequin Regency Romance™

Romance the way it was *always* meant to be!

The time is 1811, when a Regent Prince rules the empire. The place is London, the glittering capital where rakish dukes and dazzling debutantes scheme and flirt in a dangerously exciting game. Where marriage is the passport to wealth and power, yet every girl hopes secretly for love....

Welcome to Harlequin Regency Romance where reading is an adventure and romance is *not* just a thing of the past! Two delightful books a month.

Available wherever Harlequin Books are sold.